Biblioasis ~~International Transl~~**ation Series**
Gener~~al Edit~~**or: Stephen Henighan**

RED, YELLOW, GREEN

Red Yellow Green

Alejandro Saravia

Translated from the Spanish by María José Giménez

BIBLIOASIS
WINDSOR, ONTARIO

Originally published as *Rojo, amarillo y verde* by Éditions Art-Fact Press/Ediciones de la Enana Blanca, Montreal, 2003.

Copyright © Alejandro Saravia 2003

Translation copyright © María José Giménez 2017

FIRST EDITION

Library and Archives Canada Cataloguing in Publication

Saravia, Alejandro, 1962-
[Rojo, amarillo y verde. English]
    Red, yellow, green / Alejandro Saravia ; María José Giménez, translator.

(Biblioasis international translation series ; no. 20)
Translation of: Rojo, amarillo y verde.
Issued in print and electronic formats.
ISBN 978-1-77196-141-7 (softcover).--ISBN 978-1-77196-142-4 (ebook)

    I. Giménez, María José, 1977-, translator II. Title. III. Title: Rojo, amarillo y verde. English. IV. Series: Biblioasis international translation series ; no. 20

PS8587.A37656R6413 2017   C863'.64   C2017-901945-7
                                                   C2017-901946-5

Edited by Stephen Henighan
Copy-edited by Jessica Faulds
Typeset by Chris Andrechek
Cover designed by Gordon Robertson

Published with the generous assistance of the Canada Council for the Arts, which last year invested $153 million to bring the arts to Canadians throughout the country, and the financial support of the Government of Canada. Biblioasis also acknowledges the support of the Ontario Arts Council (OAC), an agency of the Government of Ontario, which last year funded 1,709 individual artists and 1,078 organizations in 204 communities across Ontario, for a total of $52.1 million, and the contribution of the Government of Ontario through the Ontario Book Publishing Tax Credit and the Ontario Media Development Corporation. Biblioasis also acknowledges the financial support of the Government of Canada through the National Translation Program for Book Publishing, an initiative of the *Roadmap for Canada's Official Languages 2013–2018: Education, Immigration, Communities,* for our translation activities.

The translator acknowledges the assistance of the Banff International Literary Translation Centre at The Banff Centre, Banff, Alberta, and the U.S. National Endowment for the Arts.

PRINTED AND BOUND IN CANADA

MIX
Paper from
responsible sources
FSC® C004071
www.fsc.org

ANCIENT FOREST ™
FRIENDLY

...to live, literally, by the story: by
a story which is nothing less than never-
ending: a sonorous, weightless edifice
in perpetual (de)construction...

Juan Goytisolo: *Makbara*

"I'm afraid of seeing you again and I want it so much. In my room I keep a flag that I dream of sending to you so you can display it on your balcony as a sign of victory over nostalgia—a sign of our thirst for ourselves—for my homeland, my country, the words I write, are you, your arms, the words you speak."[1]

Susana, I just finished shovelling the snow that was blocking the entrance to my house and now my back hurts. It's snowing and on the radio the forecast is calling for twenty more centimetres of snow. It's cold out and I don't want to leave the house, but I think I should go to the library to read—or suffer—the latest news from Bolivia brought by the handful of newspapers in Spanish that manage to reach the island of Montreal.

This morning as I started working on a story I was writing for you, I realized I had lost almost thirty pages by mistake—as a pretentious deus ex machina *would have it. They must have decided to vanish purely out of shyness and shame, imagining your gaze upon the nakedness of their distant words. If I hadn't lost them,*

---

1   *"J'ai peur de te revoir et je le souhaite si tant. Dans ma chambre je garde un drapeau dont je rêve de te l'envoyer pour que tu puisses le montrer sur ton balcon tel un signe de victoire sur la nostalgie—signe de soif de nous-mêmes—car ma patrie, ma terre, mes mots c'est toi, ta voix, tes bras, tes paroles."* Note found in an envelope returned by Canada Post ten years later to the Scribe's address in Montreal. Stained manila envelope with worn edges. Reason for non-delivery written in boldface: *"Le Kurdistan n'existe pas comme pays"* ("Kurdistan does not exist as a country"). Contents of the envelope, addressed to a woman named Bolivia, as explained by the poems at the end of this text.

I probably wouldn't be writing this convoluted letter and thinking about you. It was the kind of mistake in which a distracted, mighty finger can erase an entire city from the map, or the memory of stories yet unwritten. Susana, it's so sad to lose words this way, especially when you're a week away from turning thirty and for the occasion you have gathered all your hopes of being able to write something that will finally convince you that tracing an immigrant tongue on a piece of paper is somehow worth the trouble. Writing is so artificial, so unnecessary, compared to the practicalities of life, and yet it is so vital because one way or another, writing, this exercise of serpents, manages to merge the sum of our days into the river of words and memories. I think that's how we're born into history, a story that marks the course of our lives with a branding iron, as if Death were letting us roll the dice for a moment, just to show us how some people roll a lucky seven while others end up crucified, with their lips sewn up and their memory burning in silence. I will start over. Little by little I will rewrite the story so that you won't forget me, so I can help you remember who you were that long-gone afternoon in the Glorieta de Obrajes when we knew nothing of all this distance.

Eating Italian-inspired noodles made by Guatemalan cooks at a restaurant on Rue St-Denis, Marcelle Meyer told you with no dramatic gestures or signs of frustration, rather with an air of impassive calm, that she wanted to stop seeing you, that she had grown tired of you. You listened to her, feigning calm, and secretly regretted the absence of wine on your table, even a cheap one, to wash down that damn mouthful of potatoes that all of a sudden got stuck in your throat as if even your digestive tract was emotionally stunned by such a stabbing phrase: *"Je ne veux plus te revoir, Alfredo. Il faut se quitter. Je casse."*[2] Her voice glided with ease as it pushed the blade of separation between two ribs.

---

2   "I don't want to see you again, Alfredo. We shouldn't be together. I'm leaving you."

The next day, knowing perfectly well that it was utopian, a bad joke no one would understand, you decided to start your absurd Quechuistic project on the metro. To defy the norm, risk a possible arrest and even a not-so-unlikely prison sentence. Maybe even a few blows, as Peruvian in verse as they are heavy upon the ribs. That's how you started your day. *Monsieur, vous dérangez affreusement!*[3] A thick moustache under a cap, the uniformed metro police. Severe blue. Everything imagined. The string of metro cars stops at Jean-Talon station. The sliding doors open, fed by the powerful pulse of electricity that runs from the rivers of the cold north of Québec down into the underground bowels of this island. Passengers on a permanent journey—from the Ogooué Basin, the coronilla de Cochabamba, the ruins of Pompeii, the knives of Toledo and the bazaars of Marrakesh—they board the cars of the vast metallic intestine of the Montreal metro. They go in and out, cross paths and take in each other's eyes, coats, daytime and evening hairstyles, mouths, trousers, Turkish and Mozarabic tongues, shared air, sweat, and lotions. Shoes, sandals, winter boots. Over the bustle and noise, someone is singing the way one sings at the age of twenty.

You board the train and instinctively seek to make contact with other passengers' pupils. Iris to nerve, circular birds that take flight when they sense your gaze, dissolve into the absence of other faces and lose themselves in the epistemological depths of ads for creams, cigarettes, tickets for the baseball season, trips to lands of beaches and beach balls and palm trees, sunblock, and late-vintage wines from Arabized France. In the subways of the world, people don't make eye contact. Desires without a price tag are a threat.

---

3 "Sir, you are disturbing the peace!"

Your voice attracts the attention of other metro riders. If not because of its tone, at least because of your tongue: *"Chunquituy palomitay...kolila!"* Even if they don't understand the language, they can at least tell you're calling out for someone at the top of your lungs. Someone who will never answer. From one metro car to the next, opening forbidden latches, walking through doors in a clamorous trip through de Castelneau, du Parc, Outremont stations. *"Chunquituy palomitay...kolila!"* *Montréal est la première ville nord-américaine avec la plus grande population trilingue.*[4] The olive-skinned ears of Tamils who escaped from Jaffna's ambush and shrapnel seek familiar phonemes beneath your disguised words. A Hindu thinks he hears verses in ancient Sanskrit as he drifts in a drowsy dream towards the west end of the city after washing dishes, pots, and floors at the Bombay Palace—the palace of succulent tandoori chicken and curry sauce—with soap and scrubber in his raw hands from one in the afternoon until five in the morning at a Sainte Catherine Street restaurant. *"Chunku: n. Word that expresses love and tenderness."* You leaf through the dictionary, trying to unearth a tongue denied to you by your elders' shame and last name; they, who were so comfortable speaking it to each other in the cornfields when they didn't want to be understood by others. The Castilian Queshwa—Quechua, Wuichua, Kechua—of the forgotten Jesús Lara. The term *kolila* doesn't appear in this book. Maybe it's written with a *khu* or *ku*. Nothing. The metro keeps moving. It arrives at the next station. Doors open and close in a matter of seconds. Mechanical jaws, wooden brakes, intercourse of metal and rubber. It pulls out of Université de Montréal station. You walk through another forbidden door amidst the rattling speed

---

4   "Montreal is home to the largest trilingual population of any city in North America."

of the pneumatic ride, always searching for someone to listen, someone who will understand your stubborn muttering, someone whose earnest fingers will know how to tie the umbilical laces of your migrant Andean shoes. The passengers' eyes feign indifference as they steal glances at you. Their pupils conceal their own curiosity, or perhaps restrained reproach, disdain, perhaps racism. *Est-ce que vous êtes cuzqueño, monsieur?* You laugh. No, no, can't you see I'm a dog, *madame*? But even mongrels have a home country, don't they? *Nooo, señora! Je suis boliviano. Boliviano...boliviano! Ah!...un otro italiano!...* Ladiladaladalada... Her answer awakened in his ears the notes of an old song by the great Alfredo Domínguez, when he sang at the Radio Méndez concert hall, the notes of his guitar wafting fragrant through the speakers of the scratchy radio. The Tupizan musician had run away from home to join the circus at the age of twelve. His job was to take care of a monkey during his journey with a caravan of animals, frugal men, and hunger across the remote regions of the border between Bolivia and Argentina, regions transformed into landscapes of solitude, love and nostalgia by the exquisite strings of his guitar. Exhausted, he got off at Côte-des-Neiges station. No one had answered his plea. No one had detained him. No one had asked for explanations or accused him of breaking the rules and regulations of the public transportation service of the Greater Montreal Urban Community. As he walked towards the exit, he saw someone digging through the garbage, searching for cans of Coca-Cola or Canada Dry. An impoverished man recycling himself as a recycler. This Alfredo, Alfredo Cutipa, stood for an instant on the platform leading to the exit escalators, thinking it was best to stay in that sunless underground world—like a mineshaft in the Siglo XX mine—and realized it would be useless to expect anyone to understand the analogy, whether they spoke Quechua or not, a language to which he had no access either, despite the blood that ran through the underground tunnels beneath his skin. During the ride he had imagined the possibility of running into a *paisana* of his. If only to hear the sibilant speech again, the accent, the serpentine form of the Andean word. To be Bolivian. To have a wound that never heals. To hell with bolivia. Yes, like that, in lower case, minuscule letters for a minuscule country in the South, the most dramatic region in the world, the most...what? He couldn't find the right adjective for the immensity he wished to convey. Perplexed by his linguistic limitations, Alfredo sat down on a stone bench next to people waiting for the metro. All of a sudden, he remembered the trailer of a movie. A woman closes the door as she steps out of a small apartment building. With a snug-fitting skirt and a confident gait, she walks to a café on Place de la Contrescarpe on Rue Mouffetard. Her body and her steps merge into the crowd that makes its way down the boulevard towards the old cobblestone street. Colours are bright: it's around 11:00 on a sunny June morning, perhaps on the boulevard near Musée de Cluny. The camera rises above the pedestrians and streets in a wide-angle shot à la *Nuit américaine*, then stops facing the bar in a café packed with urbanites drinking and digesting hurried croissants dipped in steamy café au lait. She orders a croque-monsieur and *café au lait s'il-vous-plait*. Looking into the mirror on the wall behind the bar, she notices she is being followed by the eyes and broad pectorals of the hero of the movie, a resolute-looking man who asks the garçon for another coffee, then turns towards her and whispers a proposition in her ear: to spend an hour together in a nearby hotel. She looks towards the audience in the theatre, her eyes wide and amazed, as if asking for advice. Someone sitting beside me almost chokes, her saliva suddenly thick and sliding down behind her Eve's apple. The hotel receptionist's hand offers an irresistible key towards the viewer. Room 678 at the Gordon Hotel is ready for you. Every shot pregnant with uncertainty. Will she accept his carnal proposition? The screen slowly fades to black after flashing a dramatic slanted phrase at the audience: *Prochainement dans cette salle de cinéma.*[5] He opened his eyes after the dull moment of darkness, realizing all of a sudden that he was still at the Côte-des-Neiges metro station, sitting on the polished black bench next to the platform. He was sitting next to a woman who was making a discreet effort to read the title of the little book he held in his hand: Hugh MacLennan's *The Watch That Ends the Night*, a novel about a Canadian physician responsible for the first blood transplant in the history of modern medicine right in the middle of the Spanish Civil War. At the speed of a Spanish Republican bullet, Alfredo Cutipa's eyes caught her glancing at the title of his book. After an awkward moment of silence, she asked him point-blank: *"Monsieur, est-ce que vous avez vu le film?"*[6] He answered in Spanish: "No, but I'm trying to read this island by reading this book."

At night, Marcelle Meyer's face again, tired of the usual Tuesday-night movie date. After hundreds of movies, she is on the big screen of your dreams, dressed as a karate black-belt, waving her arms in a series of lethal moves as she explains in Cantonese that she doesn't want to see you any-more. And to show you how final her intentions are, she lets out a high-pitched scream, and with a brutal, well-aimed

5   "Coming soon to a theatre near you."

6   "Have you seen this film, sir?"

chop she swiftly splits open the skull of Sigmund Freud, who just sits there in his fantastic green armchair and doesn't even have time to say "¡ay!"

Laval. *Lait partiellement écrémé. Vie partiellement écrémée. Vie partiellement peuplée.* Sitting again at La Brioche Dorée, a small café packed with students and immigrants in the babelic barrio of Côte-des-Neiges—the golden *marraquetita*, the golden bun?—a quiet café with waiters whose hair is not slicked back. A small tip in exchange for this brief moment of calm, this smell of tobacco, of chess players, of distance. Between the pages of your notebook, the fading steps and image of that beggar-magician covered in shiny black grease, drinking booze out of a can, leaning against a wall on Calle Jenaro Sanjinés, muttering the chapters of a story that will never end because it hasn't yet been written.

January 1980. How did that worn copy of *Vade Mecum of the Bolivian Soldier* define Bolivia? Is Bolivia the sum of its mountains? Is it the celestial air we breathe? The flag and the national coat of arms? Is it the mother, the sister, the cousin, and the niece we beat and rape when the radios announce the coup d'état, the new military operations, the tanks and troops taking over the city sheltered in the darkness of the curfew and the sinister legitimacy of the state of siege, so impunicratically Bolivian?

Lieutenant (mestizo): "Private Mamani!"
Private Mamani (Aymara): "Yessir, Lieutenant!"
L: "Private, how do you define the Patria?"
M: "The Patria is my motherland, Lieutenant!"
L: "Very well! Private Condori! How do you define the Patria?"

Condori: "The Patria is Mamani's mother, Lieutenant!"
L: "These dumb *laris, indiosbrutoshijosdeputa*! To the sentry wall! *Hup!*"

Where did you leave that little expedition diary from 1980? In what pocket did you hide your terror, little Bolivian soldier?

Seven in the evening. Month of May. Montreal fills your lungs and you don't know whether you should read, or write, or read while writing. Better write while reading instead. Every sign, every curve on the road, every twist and circumstance becomes a step for your eyes to rise to the imagination of the past.

I wish the cheesemonger was only a cheese maker and not a butcher too!—someone cried out the slogan from the depths of your memory, a voice in a small town of quiet streets. The swollen river was rushing again through the lobes of your brain, that shocking, murky river of memories disguised in a pamphlet. "No...not again...please!" Memory: the wise queen of anarchy and intuition. Only she knows when she is leaving and when she is coming back. *After all, San Javier cheeses are not that bad.*

"Colonel...what measures will your government take to fight against the voices of the opposition?" asked the complacent featherduster from *El Diario* to the new *caudillo* of a tiny little country with no access to the Pacific Ocean, drowned in a sea of military men. "Well," answered the mouse-in-boots, trying to speak in the solemn tone of an illustrious statesman who graduated from the School of Advanced Military Studies of Bolivia, "as my meenister of de interior Mario Adett Zamora is about to esplain, we're gonna sweep out all dose evil volibianos who've tried to debase the name of our nayshon and swapped de estandar of our sanctificent motherland for de red rag of internashonalist cospirassy." The pint-sized big shot loved the sound of his own voice twenty years later as he caressed the visor of the old colonel cap that still crowned his neo-democratic bald head, an invisible cap only he could see when he looked in the mirror and considered his campaign strategy for the upcoming national elections, another war against an internal enemy. American advisors assured him that thanks to his ex-dictator skills he would definitely win. Those arduous days of his first democratic experiments in the late 1970s were long gone. A fairly difficult task to carry out from abroad, and completely futile: the masquerade would be crushed by the simple, ironclad affections of a handful of miners' and workers' wives who'd decided to stop eating one day in the month of Christmas until their men were freed from the prisons and barracks around the country. Their example spread like wildfire, and days later thousands of people poured into temples and churches in a heroic, exemplary renunciation of their mundane appetites, which until then had delighted in savouring delicious portions of fricassee, *jolke*, *anticucho*, *thimpu*, *costillar*, *boguitas*, *chairo con cuerito*, *pataska*, chicken chanka, fake rabbit, *ají mixto*, *plato paceño*, *ají de papalisa con chalona*, *charquecán*, roast goose, *majao*, *silpanchos*, *rangaranga*, *asado borracho*, *chorizos chuquisaqueños*, *tuntas* with cheese, and other delicacies from all over the vast territory of Bolivian gastronomy. And so a hunger strike started that would eventually put an end to seven years of terror. Entrenched in Plaza Murillo's Palacio Quemado, the mouse-with-epaulettes had no choice but to free the political prisoners, allow exiles to return, and hear the protests of people who were already dead, as well as promise the Bolivian people a load of crap about holding national elections.

So it was that Banzer's godson, a certain Juan Pereda Asbún, an ungrateful high-ranking air force officer, decided to stage a revolt against his godfather, he who had worked so hard filling ballot boxes with thousands upon thousands of fake votes in favour of Juanito and his puny Frente Nacional Popular. After getting drunk, that wretched godson of his tried to seize the election results and the presidential throne, all in vain. The little monkeys had failed. The fraud was so great that even two years later, in the early 1980s, the soldiers of the Air Force Security and Defence Unit—a battalion formed by eight companies of eighty-one soldiers each, plus several supernumeraries, confined at the El Alto Air Base near the city of La Paz—were still wiping their rearguard with the air force colononel's mug, the forgotten paladin whose smiling face appeared on the green ballots of the Frente Nacional Popular.

"In Bolivia, do you say colonel or colononel?" Anne and José asked while Alfredo read them these improvised passages in a tiny apartment on Fairmount Avenue, half a block from Café Kilo on Boulevard Saint-Laurent in Montreal. They could smell the bagels that were baked 24/7 in the bakery next door. Marcelle Meyer had explained to him that the sesame-covered doughnut-shaped rolls were of Jewish origin but now—a sign of our times, when marks of identity are becoming increasingly ambiguous—they were made by young olive-skinned Sri Lankan men. They rolled the little balls of dough, one under each hand, working in unison. They boiled them, dipped them in a honey-and-water solution, and coated them with sesame seeds to finally bake them for the glory and good name of the city of Montreal. He remembered this, and more, faster than a rooster can crow—though no rooster actually crowed because in Montreal there are no roosters, except the colourful plastic ones outside Portuguese restaurants. Returning to his hosts' question, Alfredo Cutipa calmly explained to them the equine logic of the uniformed in a country teeming with barracks, where it was only a matter of time before any rearguard soldier, prodded by a rifle butt, managed to climb to the top of the military hierarchy, and earned ipso facto the opportunity to take the "reins" of the nation or at least some juicy post in Customs or Narcotics. Bolivians: are they just eight, ten, fifteen, or twenty million hopelessly forgetful lambs?

What a rude question, he thought, after rereading his improvisations. And there he was again, walking down the lanes of Cala Cala, near Avenida América, his eyes searching for the century-old bark of the Great Chillijchi, father of all trees; looking for frog tracks beneath the shadow of the mighty molle trees in a faraway childhood by the Rocha River; looking for the refined elegance of a frog he could hide in his pocket and take with him to learn the gymnastics of the English language in a tiny summer school. The small amphibians never survived the linguistic experience.

Two days later, the river of words has dried up and memory sleeps the short dream of present reality. One of many possible realities. In the meantime, Marcelle Meyer, his girlfriend, had disappeared, swallowed up by the bustle of a public accounting firm, her face sprinkled with numbers and digits that wriggled like tadpoles all over her computer screen.

Drinking a bowl of café au lait at Café Le Damier on Saint-Denis and Bélanger, he thought that he, Alfredo Cutipa, would never get anywhere if he kept wandering around carrying the weight of his personal history on his back, as if he were some *aparapita* carrying a grand piano, chewing his *acullico* of coca and *llipta*, drenched in sweat, climbing up the steep Calle Pisagua in La Paz. Where were these fictions taking him?

If you don't believe me, ask Ponciano Villca. He wouldn't let me lie. Ask him how many high-ranking soldiers, from the second echelon, came that night in February of 1980 to break our souls with all the rage accumulated over 300 days and nights of ser-vicious military service. They came in through the broken windows facing the barracks at the main point of entry to the military base on El Alto's Avenida 16 de Julio. I'm not talking about the avenue of the same name in downtown La Paz—a gaudy, pompous, frivolous circuit used as catwalk by a sector of the population that tries to hide their *indio* nails, their *indio* names, their collective mestizo memory ashamed of the blood in their veins. I mean this one here, this wide Avenida 16 de Julio in El Alto, this one teeming with *indios*, stinking of the frantic sweat and concrete of bricklayers and the mouldy tobacco of construction workers who will drink *agua de sultana* until they die, this avenue that smells of the rough grass and coca of the Aymaras who've just arrived in the city, future bricklayers, future construction workers, future *aparapitas*, future drunkards and market *caseritas*, future flags for the Inter-American Development Bank and its desperate attempt to show how modern the small-business *cholitas* are as they fight slowly but surely against hunger, selling their *aji de fideo* for one peso, fake rabbit with rice and *llajua*, fresh rack of puppy-lamb with a side of steaming *chorrellana* and boiled potatoes, while their children wander from corner to

21

corner shining shoes, selling candles, *marraquetas*, screws, calculators madeinChina, and flypaper.

"Alfredo, are you still serving up that same old commie speech from the seventies?" asks the Scribe, who keeps track of every single one of my words, jotting them down in his notebook with great care. "How much longer, che!"

The Scribe licks the tip of the pencil he is using to write these lines. An avid follower of the writing ritual, he thinks any text can end up becoming the next Holy Bible. He looks at me, waiting for the next word, the next sentence. Even though he doesn't agree with me and loathes these words, he knows that the story must keep moving, twisting around like an earthworm in the vast humus of Bolivian collective identity. Impossible to fix, preserve or restrain. I'll keep telling my story about that night. Without turning on the lights in the giant troop barracks, the high-ranking soldiers entered, their faces covered, and ordered us to jump out of our narrow four-tier bunk beds. They wrenched us out of sleep in the dark and ordered us to form a line, which ended up more crooked than an *achachi* dancer's staff because of our fear. Later on we learned there were only four of them, all from a tiny village in the Altiplano near the lake, but at the time, the accumulated rage of those beaten Natives would have been enough to fill Lake Titicaca with blood.

"¡Ya, *ferme carajo!*... ¡Fermeydichu mono y mierdas!" they ordered us, keeping their voices lowered, feeling powerful, violent and methodical.

Thuds, fists pounding ribs and faces, someone's breath bursts into a whimper or groan at a blow to the stomach. A shadow bends over and crumples to the floor at El Alto's military garrison. Someone starts crying, quietly. Alfredo breathes nervously, listening. His sweaty hands shake like two fish on land. The air in his ears swells at the crack of a slap near his face. Everything happens in the dark, almost in silence. There are no faces or names, no one to call on, no hand intervenes to stop the fury of a night as dark as a black whale swollen with bile.

"Stop...please stop...please!" someone cries out before collapsing to the ground, rolling and folding under the kicks and blows.

We couldn't break formation. We were nailed to the floor—perhaps by our incipient military discipline, perhaps by fear. As I tried to figure out what time it was, fervently wishing for the first light of sunrise, I felt my mouth explode and, before I was even aware of the pain, hot blood running down my chin. I fell back, shocked by the silent attack, ears ringing, lips throbbing, unable to make sense of what was happening in that space where shadows moved and foul breath whispered bitter orders all around me.

"You're making that up! That's cheap literature, che, like those little pamphlets written by the resistance where the heroic militant smiles like Superman while someone rips his nails out or slices him open and hangs his guts out to dry. You're pulling my leg, che! This Alfredo is really something else...You'll never change!"

"No, no, Scribe!... I swear it's true! Ask Ponciano Villca, he remembers, he was there. He wouldn't let me lie."

The Scribe shook his head in resignation and kept writing as Alfredo dictated, since that was his job.

They were sitting around a table at La Bruja, a dive bar in a dusty narrow street at the foot of the Ceja de El Alto, in the city of La Paz. The bar had several small patios with chairs and covered tables crowned with giant pitchers of chicha. Alfredo and his buddies, now civilians who had completed their military service, saw a group of former soldiers from who-knows-which battalion walk up to a nearby table. They had a guitar and a fat pitcher of chicha. For some reason, maybe the way they walked, Alfredo surmised they had been infantry soldiers. They'd had enough to drink to shed their Andean timidity with regard to emotions, and now showed a mix of cheerful despair and the sadness of *Pepinos* without a carnival. It was as if they were drinking their first chicha after a year of compulsory military service "in the heart of the Armed Farces, as established by the Political Constipation of the State," said Alfredo Cutipa with improvised solemnity watching them approach. He even felt as if he and his army mates had been in the same military unit, the same regiment, the same army, with the men sitting beside them. The newcomers plucked a song by Domínguez out of the air and their voices and eyes plunged off-key into that cadence of guitar strings concocted by the Tupizan into a song that no one in the world except soldiers could truly understand:

> Who knows what affections
> spin around in his mind
> our Private Juan Cutipa,
> while he's cleaning his guns,
> our Private Juan Cutipa.

The guitars and voices—some deep, some high-pitched—of teenagers branded by violence with the white-hot iron of coups d'état and the silent, anguished gestures of the 1979 and 1980 corpses gradually grew quiet and sank with their hearts into the lyrics of the song that came to life in their hands, in their voices, eyes, and souls. Surprised, the boys felt the tears that welled up in their throats now rising to their eyes like frightened, shiny fish, softening the leathery skin on cheeks that had faced the fire and ice of the Bolivian Altiplano. Some of them started to cry, trying to hide their tears, ashamed of what they considered a clear sign of diminished virility, their heads bowed, quiet tears falling on their worn veterans' boots.

"Here, here," said the Scribe, reaching out towards him, "it's all right...calm down, man, it's over..."

Alfredo stretched out his hand and grabbed the wrinkled handkerchief offered by the Scribe, still recognizing himself in those ex-soldiers.

"You still remember these things, Alfredo?"

"Yes, I remember, Scribe. That's why you're here, to help me gouge out of my eyes, to find out if I can forget all this by writing it down."

Yes, Ponciano remembers that night. How many Bolivians does this story belong to? Why is the wheel of uniforms and humiliation still turning? In the end, we would just laugh and choose to take the rage and violence with humour, and even a touch of nostalgia; because it was the type of violence that made you feel completely detached from your aggressors, your little bosses, your *excelentísimos* who would be just that for the rest of your life. Because that's how they turned us into real men. But did they really make us manlier? By taming us to just take the pain? By making us comfortable with resignation and numb to violence? Come on, brother, let's piss on the Bolivian flag, on the political constitution of the state, on the historical constipation that orders us to be patriotic and serve the country. But whose country? Being patriotic means letting others kick you, letting them beat you up and insult you. So deeply patriopic, aren't we? These *soldaditos*...

these little patriopic *bolivianitos*... They're just so nice. And that's exactly why they deserve it.

In the middle of Quinta La Bruja, in a lower-class barrio in El Alto. After the song ended, plunging the guys at the next table into a pensive mood, Alfredo stood up, inspired by the noble but mean Incan liquor that would leave him with a respectable head-throbbing *chaqui* the next day. A chicken thinking himself a tenor, he burst into song with the national anthem: *"Boliviaaaassnos helaaaaados propiciooos, coronoooo...coronooooo...coronoooo..."* He got stuck in that word, forgetting what came next, both delighted and horrified that he might have forgotten the sacrosanct rhythm. Someone yanked him by the arm, forcing him to sit back down.

"Shut up, you dickhead! The cops are gonna take us in! You haven't changed much, have you... Fucking commie!"

"Well, like the man said it: let's go impregnate our hens, brother!"

Ten years later, a poem by a Tarijan man who left his homeland—and returned ten years later to find that his people looked at him with emptiness in their eyes—landed on a blank page as he started to write a letter, not knowing quite how to start the first line but thinking of Susana San Miguel, all dressed in black, sitting on a white sofa, her hair long and shiny, so long that it had reached across thousands of days and kilometres, mountain ranges, family tragedies, customs inspectors, and ruthless Canadian winters, all the way to where he was, and managed to bring warmth to his fingers again, the fingers that were now writing her: *Susana, I just finished shovelling the snow that was blocking the entrance to my house and now my back hurts. It's snowing and on the radio the forecast is calling for twenty more centimetres of snow. It's cold out and I don't want to leave the house, but I should go to the library to read—or suffer—the latest news from Bolivia brought by the handful of newspapers in Spanish that manage to reach the island of Montreal.*

"I used to be president, and a man who reaches that government seat of honour would never set out to deceive his people. You take on an enormous responsibility up there, and you absolutely cannot, ever, lie to the people." He felt sonorous, filled with something that resembled happiness, picturing the road to power wrapped around his temples like a crown of Caesarean laurels. At last the dusty colononel could answer without a shred of doubt the journalists' questions about his seven years in power—no need to mentally prepare to explain and lessen the weight of the dead and the exiles. He no longer needed to give half-hearted explanations about the nepotistic fate of the accrued debt or hide the conditions that had made him president of a country fractured into various coexisting societies, languages and historical times. Later that day, the former colononel ordered one of his assistants to kindly suggest to newspapers that the word "president" be capitalized. Pretty please. He then called the then-president-in-office, a certain Jaime Paz, a manling more cunning than Caco, nephew of another president, a despot of an old man and lover of manoeuvres and bayonets in his spare time. Now, forced by political convenience and the ever-shrinking weight of the dead, Jaime Paz had become a friend—in fact, the old tyrant considered him almost a son. An opponent of the colononel's dictatorship after the coup d'état of August 1971, and having endured the hardship of exile and persecution, by mid-1985 he had finally revealed a trait that would distinguish him and his people: a stubborn, instinctive, animal ambition lacking any talent whatsoever. The first thing Jaime Paz did as soon as he became vice-president was to devote himself to sabotaging and plotting against his own regime, a coalition united under the name of Unión Democrática y Popular, led by Hernán Siles Suazo, until— not a speck of remorse, forget that—he finally set out to co-govern in kleptocratic union with his ex-exiler.

Old colononel Banzer thought that in 1993 or in 1997, or even after his death, no one would question the illustrious place he would occupy in national history textbooks once he was democratically elected president of either a republic or hell. On the intercom next to his massive mahogany desk, he asked not to be disturbed and called on his assistants—who were lounging around in the next room—to take his messages, he wasn't there if anyone called. He took out his dentures, gave his tired gums a slow tongue massage and closed his eyes, picturing the next 6th of August—a date that in happier days would have caused prolonged erections and military parades—feeling almost the same excitement he felt the day he graduated from Colegio Mingidor Gualberto Villarroel. Submerged in old black-and-white memories, he suddenly opened his eyes after feeling a swift, light touch, a presence in the air, as if on one side of the room he had again glimpsed the fourteen shadows that used to file by one by one in his worst sleepless hours. No, he wouldn't let those corpses found by accident in a mass grave at the La Paz cemetery disturb him. He wouldn't allow them, not now. Fucking dead. That's what you get for being commies. Shoulda known better. It's your fault, you damn *wakabolas*, that I haven't slept a wink in more than twenty years. And if he did he kept his eyes open. That's how he cheated the spectres of the disappeared. When they saw his eyes, they thought he was awake and didn't bother him. He called on one of his assistants with the voice of a troop commander and ordered, "Bring me some *ají de fideos a la marinera!*" His carnal dagger demanded engagement in a new penetration campaign against the carnal red forces that were always there where you least expected them.

How to stop the rivers of time and memory from flooding and washing out to the sea of dying what little love we may have left? By searching, by inventing María, the one who returns to the South with a *charango* and a letter. Not Death.

I have decided to look for you here and I don't even know how. I've seen you in so many faces and I don't even know if it's because of these lines that I'll succeed in recognizing you. You said it would be difficult, if not impossible, to have you here. I am scared of finding you and realizing that perhaps it was futile to travel down this long road half-devoured by years of wanting. I also know that when I finally reach you I will have to put a face on you, name you, fill you with shapes, desires and silences. And I don't even know how I will manage to do that. Today I've decided to look for you here and I can't think of more beautiful words to start my day.

The best way to start will be to let traces of you inhabit me. I will fill myself with your gestures, your capital letters. I will see a street. Stare at a café in the corner. The tables. This key on my keyboard. A handkerchief falling on the ground as the metro goes by. A scream near the bridge at dawn. The hum of an accordion as I wander through the Old Port. A page torn from a book, asleep between the pages of another. Then I will look in the mirror and say that you were here for a moment and I'm finally holding a sign of you, that at last I have you in some way.

I hadn't thought about that in a long time, finding a page from one book resting in the embrace of another. I think you mentioned it the night we met and you sat next to me at a café on Chemin de la Reine-Marie months ago, or was it years ago?

Sometimes I lose track of you and I hate you and I get tired of looking for you in vain. And I tell myself that the night belongs only to you—the night, where you take all and none of the forms that exist. I close my eyes and think of your lips, my hands recognize your body. You're lying back, eyes half-closed, giving and denying me the little death that hides behind the mask of joy and pleasure. Then the anguish of knowing everything is finite, that all our haste and desire did nothing but spur the voracity of time. And then I know I have lost you, and I know myself to be too rough, drunk on my fears, awkward like a blind animal, unable to recognize the lightness of your leaving.

I start over. I find a name for you: María. And then I invent an encounter, always the first, always the same one, where my eyes converse with your fingers and your voice touches me and your laughter undresses me. We turn serious, take some distance, know ourselves to be secret accomplices in what you call an exercise in desire and I name the desire of invention. Then our voices touch, caress, recognize each other across the night and the distance. They play and chase and own each other and make promises. My voice sleeps with you and your hair shows me the way into the night that sleeps upon your breasts, into the primeval waters of your pubis, into the eye of life eternal.

Always in you,
Alfredo.

The only way to explain what it means to be Bolivian is through violence. It is as though that first blast of air that welcomes us into the Andean world at birth slowly became punches, sticks, stones and bullets. Nothing else could explain that sense of normalcy, the daily and brutal manifestations of a viceroyal democracy in an endless paper-and-cardboard performance, donning convenient disguises as needed—bayonet, barracks, congress. Bolivia: a colony of civil dictators and important frogs where the exercises of violence invade even the tiniest spaces between flesh and nail.

The worn-out colononel had always thought the art of seduction belonged to the republic of civilians. Especially to that pretentious middle class, men who in his view became lesser men as soon as they set foot in a university and started choosing what colour tie to wear—if they were in finances—or grew a beard that always hid a disgusting Marxist camouflaged under the title of sociologist. Morons. At that precise moment in the year of our Lord Jesus Christ one thousand nine hundred and seventy-one, the Gasser family—or some other similar family of important agro-industry landowners, acting in the name and representation of people of good family name and better bank accounts—had a big fat package delivered to the mouse-in-boots-and-battle-fatigues. A package of patriotic, necessary dollars set aside as funds to rectify the course of the nation, which was dangerously set on the tortuous paths of the international left. This, thanks to the complicity of a bad military man and even worse Bolivian, General Juan José Torres González, who would later be assassinated, several shots to the back of the head from some decent patriotic members of the Argentinian Triple A screaming "Death to the Bolivian!" under a Buenos Aires bridge. The young, rampant colononel Hugo Banzer didn't need to put on a tie or fake civil intellidumbness to sell the powers of his efficacy to his importer patrons, his agro-industrial uncles and his banking and mining friends. He had the necessary credentials to seduce the illustrious Bolivian bourgeoisie—his first failed military uprising, the lethal wisdom he'd acquired from the gringos who taught at the School of the Americas, and his austere military boots. And his name, his name: Hugo Banzer, a booming, iron-cross name with a metallic buzz that echoed German tanks razing the last Polish defences, or tanks coming down from El Alto at 4:00 AM to storm the dream palace of all Bolivians. But nothing had prepared him for his greatest hour of glory, when in 1988 he was honoured by the highest accolade his name, "General Hugo Banzer," could ever receive: entering the Hall of Fame of his old School of the Americas, buried in the heat and humidity of Georgia, Southern state and old bastion of slavery during the American Civil War. This prestigious distinction granted by the mightiest empire was only earned by the best, the most diligent students from the most important of all the important military schools. Next to such a magnanimous act of public recognition—performed in English—having a dusty avenue in the city of Santa Cruz named after him seemed to be such an unsophisticated tribute—in Spanish—from his naïve, sentimental, amnesiac countrymen.

June of 1993 was only four hours away and carried enough loneliness and nostalgia to chill Alfredo Cutipa to the bone, as though he was standing naked waiting for the train at the Charaña station.

Marcelle Meyer had left him again, the last time, and taken with her all her memories, her voice and her books. And her shoulders—moon apples, skin eyes that had gazed at him with utmost calm and affection in perfect, intimate dawns together on Rue Cartier that would never return.

Alfredo wrote down in his little madeinChina notebook that the Bolivian presidential elections would be happening in a few days. The carnival season was approaching—a farce performed in a viceroyalty that dreamed itself sovereign, independent and with a national anthem. A colony with its own army of self-occupation. In those months, he read the news with growing disquiet, examined the rhetorical masks worn by characters playing in the fatuous exercise, the potential viceroys' empty promises. Bolivians had so much faith in them, the same people who had profited from the dictatorship feasts. Bolivians listened, attentive and eager, besieged day after day by the fangs of hunger and unemployment, urged by the blindest of hopes to believe in something, someone, anyone.

The masked ball was attended by former colononel Banzer, his condor claws still caked with dried blood—not his own. He was eager to become president and held the wishful thinking that twenty-two years was enough for the bones of people killed under the Banzerate to disintegrate and stop screaming underground. "If you are really quiet, you can still hear their little bones singing, *generalito* Banzer... They'll always be right under your bed, singing just for you. Manchay Puito's femur, for example. The bones of the dead will keep singing and wailing, especially in August, month of winds, month of the dead and memories that never go away." These lines, mailed with no sender address, reached the hands of *generalisisisísimo* Banzer on November 1, 1987. The sender was clearly someone in the opposition, some little shit with nothing better to do than pester a good democrat and better patriot. Someone in the family, he thought, an insolent nephew who wanted to cleanse the family name. Not a lot of people know the mailing address of the Great Marshal of Oblivion, the favoured son of Bolivia's perfumed kleptocracy.

Hugo Banzer, in a small sitting room in the hundred-year-old sombre mansion, was shaking his head, lamenting again his former excess of patriotic fervour. He never should have staged his military coup in August, month for celebrating the nation's independence and the theatrics and hyperbolic affronts of imaginary heroes and unrelenting warriors as magnificent as any Amadís de Gaula in a chivalric romance. He should have planned his coup during the carnivals, in February. That way, he said to himself, between the protests and the processions, many Bolivians would have focused instead on fiestas, dances, *singani* and urgent orgasms. That way, the memory of bullets piercing the wind—shootings from military airplanes against the Universidad Mayor de San Andrés, against the civilian resistance at the foot of the Laikakota hill that August afternoon in 1971—that memory would have been less jarring, less annoying. His enemies—who rinsed their mouth everyday with words like justice, memory and human rights—would have seen their acts of remembrance and their stupid dead drowning in the indifference of the holiday and its water balloons, *challas* and drunkenness. What do they know about how hard it is to save a country from Castro-communism? he thought. What do they know about what it means to be Bolivian?

The other masked guest was a businessman more efficient than forty bilingual thieves trained in Chicago. Gonzalo Sánchez de Lozada spoke perfect, fluent English and a shameful Spanish in a country where around half of the population spoke Quechua, Aymara or other languages. Intellectually domesticated in the United States, he still had good contacts at the Inter-American Development Bank, the Instant Misery Fund and the World Bank. Incidentally, he was well-loved by people who wrote for the *New Yorker*, a weekly magazine published at number 20 on West 43rd street in the maze that is New York. They also spoke highly of him at the *Economist*, a conservative magazine published in Europe—the same Europe that invented the charms of modern warfare, where in 1932 Mauser rifles were manufactured in smaller sizes to fit hypothetically invincible Bolivian soldiers, overpriced rifles for an absurd war fought in the Chaco sands. Same people, same thieves, different masks. The Bolivian bourgeoisie: stingy and stinky and fattened on money, hopelessly barren of ideas, always cornered into a ménage-à-trois and submitting to boots, then to ties, or both at the same time. Bolivian bourgeoisie: a big word you fail to live up to, and your newspapers are so bad!

He woke up and searched all over his room. He opened his drawers. Looked under the bed. Opened his armoire. Nothing. No trace. It had been raining all night and the branches in the wind sounded as if they were laden with fragile green birds shaking their wings to dry. Until last night, it had been sitting in the middle of his bedroom like an antique piece of furniture you don't dare get rid of, a family heirloom that's always in your way. He went to the kitchen and looked for it in his cooking pots. He opened the fridge—the light in the appliance revealed a half-eaten piece of cheese, vegetables waiting for the final judgment, a piece of chicken still looking pale after its most recent experience, and some pears and apples having a board meeting. It wasn't there either. He couldn't even find a trace of it. He was sure he'd seen it at the foot of the bed, where it usually was when he went to sleep. Most of the time it just stayed there, coiled like an old toothless viper. Other times it would turn into a feral cat or a third shoe for some invisible foot that turned up on the street in cities he visited, guiding his footsteps along paths and alleys he never wanted to take. But this morning it was gone. He walked up to the window that looked out over Montreal, pondering the remote possibility that it might have jumped from the ninth floor. No. It was too high. Finally he surrendered to the evidence. He was alone, unable to ask anyone any questions. Hatred was gone, at last.

You won't be able to ask Boxeador anything. He won't be able to tell you because the virtue of bones is silence. Even if you run through the night tripping on uneven ground and rough grass until you reach that lost point in the Altiplano where two men are looking for each other in the dark with knotted fists, screaming in the voice of blood that never sleeps. You can hear it, the thud of a fist on the other man's flesh, bones and blood. You witness every fall, your nose feels the dust in the air from two bodies rolling around in the dirt like two fighting fish running aground. You are the frozen witness, the invisible actor in the fight, unable to stop or lessen the weight of violence. Here, at guard post number eleven at the El Alto military base, here, almost midnight, under a sky heavy with luminous pulsations and black stars, here where Vicios and Boxeador seek each other's fists and blood, here you are the witness, which is also a way to be an actor. They split up for a moment, as if to fill their lungs again. You hear them panting. Little by little their tired lungs cloud their judgment and memory, make them lose sight of who's attacking and who's defending, who's offending and who's offended. It doesn't matter. Their sweaty feet in soldier boots test the ground again, looking for a firm stance but also hoping to win over the earth, to earn its sweetness for when it's time to fall. In that mess of uniforms attacking and shredding the other, the voice of one contender spits at the other: "Damn you! You...you were there that night, too! It's your fault, too, damn you!" The rage in his words is a ball of rancid lard stuck in his throat, concentrated deep in his chest, something that screaming won't help dissolve or disappear. Each word a slingshot crashing against the crystal of the night. Again the fighters fall down twisted around each other like ants, one red, one black, pulling on hair and ears and scratching at each other.

Vicios is taller, more mestizo than *indio*, more beer drinker than chicha drinker compared to Boxeador, who's shorter, dark-skinned and broad-shouldered with a stocky neck. His head seems to sprout right from between his shoulders, his arms heavy like two pendulums. His nose shows signs of having been broken more than once. Beneath his Spanish you can hear some intonations, some vowels pronounced a certain way that reveal—like the foundations of colonial churches built with stones from the ancient Puma Punku or Tiahuanaco constructions—that he also speaks Aymara. Boxeador came from Santiago de Machaca to become a real man, as they say in the communities in the Altiplano. Or maybe from Guaqui, who knows—*quén sabe*, like the Aymara say when they speak Spanish, *quén sabe*.

In the distance, the city lights roll up the hillsides of the *hoyada paceña*, the cradle that is La Paz. Up here, on the high plateau between the mountain ranges, there is no light. To see if there are soldiers approaching on their night rounds, you have to lie down and look out level with the ground. In that narrow space between the earth and the darkness you can see a dim trickle of light, a pale halo radiating from the ground. Welterweight stance, fists tight shielding his face, eyes sharp looking for a target—Boxeador moves in, feints and retreats like a tragic dancer. His threatening knuckles pump the air in slow deliberate cycles, facing Vicios, whose sweaty, white-knuckled fists flap randomly, clutching a radio battery in each hand to give his blows more weight. A fist bursts through the shadows, aimed at the other fighter's face, and then an explosion of enraged bats erupts, fists rise, burst lips, sink into ribs, break teeth, flatten noses and swell eyelids and eyebrows. In one blow, time falls flat and frozen on the ground, its retinas burst. In one blow you fall down, too, blood coming out of your mouth, no idea where it came from or who threw the punch.

"*Bolivia es una patria imaginaria*. A territory that doesn't exist beyond a contradictory geography that contains all the labyrinths and infernos we cling to, desperate to find an end, a meaning, almost two hundred years after its birth and death occurred at the foot of the same mountains, the same jungles and forests, the same doubts and the same tragedies. It is our collective way of imagining ourselves and dying that unite us."

He felt as if his blood, the same blood he'd used to write the above lines, had suddenly dried up. Alfredo Cutipa reread the lines he had just so pompously penned. He reflected on his attempt to conjure up the homeland that chased him in his dreams—wrapped in a long white sheet serving as a classical *peplos*—and he realized it was all a futile contortion aimed at renouncing his origins. And yet he persisted in trying to erase the minuscule channels the tricolour knife had opened on his fingertips. Identity lines the patria had carved on his skin. Fingerprints stamped one day on a Bolivian passport on a one-way journey. That Patria had the sallow face of a woman, flaccid cheeks, one flat breast exposed and completely dried up. The Patria turned up again on the city streets by the deed and grace of little *llockallitas* wearing ragged shorts and espadrille *abarcas* on their feet. Officers of the Ministry of Information had paid the children six *marraquetas* a day to run through the streets of La Paz, paste and brush in hand, to put up posters printed on giant four-colour sheets of paper. The propaganda of then-minister of finance Gonzalo Chanchos de Lodaza (or Pigs-in-the-Mud), declaimed the patriotically unavoidable need to tighten our intestines and accept the new draconian, brutal, efficient, pragmatic, lucid, modern, postmodern and global economic measures they had used to paper the crumbling adobe-and-brick walls of La Paz. A hopeless effort. It would take troops, tanks and three consecutive state-of-siege decrees to convince millions of Bolivians to stay poor and without a passport for the good of the Patria. *"Ehs pour ell beeayn day tohdows,"* said future president Chanchos de Lodaza smiling for the TV cameras, a few months before he became one of the most important mining exporters in the country after his outrageous appropriation of the nation's mines.

In the middle of the night, unable to sleep again, Alfredo thought about the very real possibility that Patria, the woman pictured on the dusty posters of yesteryear, had somehow managed to sneak into his suitcase and travel with him from La Paz to Montreal just to disrupt his sleep. Freshly printed on the walls of the Illimanesque city of his dreams was the image of the Madre Patria, the Motherland, watching over him with that incurable sadness in her eyes from her world of flags and hasty inks. At the bottom of the poster, by way of explanation, an absurd slogan: *Bolivia: export or die*, or perhaps, *Son, help me by paying your taxes*, or was it the draft for compulsory military service? In a corner of his memory, he heard "When the Patria calls, even a mother's cry falls silent"—it was Carlos Paricollo, non-commissioned officer of the Bolivian Armed Forces, confidently drilling to his soldiers, tying his shiny boots, sharpening his bayonet, always sniffing the air for a chance to shoot in a new fake war. He tried to stop thinking about the woman-symbol of his country, pondering the words he planned to start writing at daybreak, but his brain resembled a Platonic cavern, a remote outside world he had no access to, with voices and shadows projected on the walls from bodies that kept chasing each other around and confusing him. Where were those words coming from, startling him awake for no reason? Lying awake, his light on in his room on the ninth floor of Rue de Maisonneuve near metro Guy, Alfredo again repeated the old words that kept him awake: "*...girondinos modernos, ¡oh patriotas!, nunca olvidéis las postreras notas del que al morir se envuelve en su bandera...*"[7] Words recited in kindergarten during a faraway daily civics ritual now floated to the surface of the early morning hours, a log submerged for a long time, eaten away by microscopic years.

After exhausting all possible explanations, Alfredo was convinced that the woman he was seeing emerge stealthily out of the dark and walking towards his bed was indeed Patria. He felt her firm gaze upon him; the figure hardly made a sound. She sat on the edge of the bed and stared at him for a long time. Alfredo felt her body slide underneath the sheets and snuggle up to him, heard her whisper anthems in his

7   "...Modern Girondins, oh patriots! Never forget the last words uttered by he who on his deathbed wrapped himself in the flag..."

ear, her cold stubborn feet seeking the warmth of his bash-ful Andean body. It was two in the morning. He pinched himself to check if he was actually awake and groped in the dark for the lamp on his bedside table. In the harsh light of truth, Alfredo Cutipa was startled to see the inexplicable flesh-and-blood presence of a body next to his. Regaining his composure, he tried to comfort himself thinking he had somehow entered a deeper phase of sleep and was now in one of those dreams where contours are as clear and sharp as to almost reproduce exactly what we call reality. Sheltered by this thought, he felt daring enough to address the intruder in his bed:

"Your feet are so cold. Would you like some socks? Someone sent me a pair of wool socks from Bolivia for the winter."

He swallowed hard, thinking his offer was out of order. It sounded phony—usually in dreams there are no verbal conversations. The cues of meaning lie in your intuitions, in the mental dialogue found only in the logic of the dream world.

"No, thanks. I have a tuque," Patria answered in a low voice, pointing with a look of resignation to the bright red cap on her head.

"That's not a sleeping cap. It's the famous Phrygian cap, isn't it?"

"No, no, it's for the cold. It's all the same in the end."

He thought it was odd to find himself in bed with Patria, the Motherland, although taking a better look, more than mother Patria she looked more like daugh-ter Patria. The dream scene was absurd, even heretical. He thought it wouldn't be wise to recount the details of the situation to his fellow countrymen on the island where he lived. If the patriotic members of Montreal's

Bolivian Residents' Association ever found out, they might not even let him back into the bazaar they held every August 6th, day of *salteñas*, *anticuchos* and other happy gastronomic nationalisms washed down with generous amounts of Labatt and Molson—which according to experts had nothing on the quality and flavour of the Paceña Blonde that never lies—a day when everyone is everyone else's brother and people treat each other to food and drinks: *"hermanitoy... servite pues, che... un sequito..."* Alfredo snapped out of the national feast scene and leaned back more comfortably on his pillow against the headboard. The woman did the same. They stayed there for a while, arms crossed, eyes fixed on an invisible point on the wall in front of them.

Alfredo looked at the time. The intruder fixed the red hat she was wearing to keep her head warm.

"You don't sleep?" Alfredo asked.

"I'll go to sleep when you do, che."

"I'll turn the light off if you want."

"No! Don't turn it off! Please leave it on. It looks just like the torch Pedrito Domingo lit for me as his declaration of love before he was hanged the summer of 1810. It was January. The 26th, I think. Or was it in 1985? Hmm. Now that I think about it I don't really know exactly when it happened. Oh, I do know there's a lovely painting at the museum on Calle Jaén. Do you remember? It's a romantic oil painting. Pedro is in it, thinking about me. His moustache is sharp, so elegant and stern. Did you see how they fixed up his house? They did a gorgeous job, with a fountain in the middle of the patio. And the floors! Oh, the floors! Spotless and waxed, just the way I like them. The house would look great in one of those interior design magazines. *Ay!* You people of the Andes are always so melodramatic about things! You only remember the hanging but not the soirées Pedrito would have at the house on Calle Jaén. We had so much good chicha!"

It seemed to him that Patria's view of national history was somewhat unhinged, so he thought it wiser not to ask any more questions. He looked on his nightstand for something to read. He found a thin copy of *Serpent Exercises*, a manual to improve your breathing from A to Z, with guaranteed results. He realized right away there was no way he could practise all those exercises to stay in shape. He sighed and noticed the woman's eyes still fixed on him. They stared at each other for a long time, not knowing what to say to each other, keeping to themselves, until Alfredo Cutipa started babbling like a nervous wind-up monkey with cymbals and all:

"I would like to kindly say, I mean, well, let's just drop all formalities, I just want to say, and it's not because of a thorn on my side or anything, but I'm up to here with that whole thing about you being my mother, doña Patria. I'm fucking done with it. I want you to get this once and for all: you're not my mother and I'm not your son. I hope I'm not offending you or making you feel like your life is worthless or anything."

"I know," she replied with a look of indifference that Alfredo mistook for resignation, "and that doesn't make me more or less worthy. I am *la Patria*. Period. And I could be your grandmother, your lover, your friend, your great-grandmother, your sister-in-law, your employee, your enemy, your wife, your sister, your daughter, your mother, your death, your granddaughter, your daughter-in-law, your cousin, your whore, your secretary, your niece, your mother-in-law, your aunt or even your cat or your dog if you want. It's all the same to me."

Hearing her response, Alfredo Cutipa sat up on the bed, embarrassed and shocked, and stared at her in disbelief.

"Tell me," she went on, "do you have any cigarettes in this inn?"

"No, I don't have any. But wait, weren't you raped by colonels and generals every time there was a coup? Didn't you suffer beyond words at the hands of that pack of kleptomaniacs, dipsomaniacs, megalomaniacs and coke dealers that were the Barrientos, Banzer, Natusch, García Meza, Chanchos de Lodaza and Paz Zamora, not to name the ones who keep sucking your blood and the ones waiting for their turn? Hadn't the entire middle class waited in line to take turns on top of you, like that woman in *Last Exit to Brooklyn*? Didn't you almost starve to death in the Llallagua and Siglo XX mineshafts? Isn't the massacre still continuing today thanks to the gringos in the Yungas and Chapare?"

The words kept pouring out, tripping over each other like moviegoers leaving a theatre in flames. He would have kept talking but she cut him off and articulated every single cold, brutal word:

"You know nothing! You have no idea what you're talking about, you runaway piece of shit! Just shut up and go to sleep! Men tend to be more tolerable when they're asleep and not snoring or bugging anyone…"

He felt as if he'd just been hit by a brick, so he just listened, stunned.

"Don't you know that there are as many Bolivias as there are Bolivians? There are seven, eight, ten, twenty millions of patrias and more. Everyone has their own, imaginary or real, thin or fat, young or old, male or female, and they are all called Bolivia but they're not the same. Only naïve people like you who swallowed up all the stories told in Civics class actually think there is only one single Patria. Besides, what's the difference between patria and country?"

"Well, they're also names of newspapers, right?"

She shot him a sour look. Alfredo saw it wouldn't help him much to try to be funny. It wouldn't make a difference at all. Would he need to give a structural answer? (And here the two scribes in charge of editing and proofreading this text couldn't agree on the proper term. While eating Lebanese olives, they shot suggestions back and forth as if they were discussing a delectable dessert—a ping-pong game of rich signifiers like post-structuralist, neostructuralist, generativegrammarborealtransformational, etc. They finally settled for sociocritical as the most suitable theoretical framework to explain the difference between patria and country, even though, considering the oneiric aspects of the situation, a psychoanalytical approach could be more fruitful, both semantically and ideologically. To celebrate their choice, the scribes mutually pledged, if they ever had the chance in the next world, they would do their best and their worst to devour—properly seasoned and charcoal-grilled—anyone who dares try to interpret this cannibalistic passage. Happy as lambs, they laughed and laughed throwing theoretical fragments and pits at each other.) Impassive, she waited for an answer. He looked at her again, not knowing what to say, until Patria spoke again in a softer tone:

"To begin with, Alfredo, tell me, my sweet Alfredito, are you sure I am a woman? A patria can be so many things, even a chair, a typewriter, a computer, an immigrant's suitcase under the bed, a photo from kindergarten..."

Alfredo hesitated at the question, trying to understand what she meant. As he searched for the answer, and unaware of where his eyes wandered, he suddenly found himself staring at Patria's breasts through her peplum. They now seemed more—how shall we put it—more convincing than before. Looking at Patria's body, Alfredo gradually and unwittingly forgot every search, answer and argument he'd had, and reached out his hand towards her breasts, feeling as if he were crossing an odd border through the sheets. A buzzing sensation ran through his body, a slow electric current reaching higher and higher voltage. He turned towards her and started caressing her soft skin under the thin cloth. His hand slowly reached the glorious summit of a nipple, which upon contact with his fingers awoke and stood up, curious to know whether the forecast called for snow that day. Alfredo couldn't help thinking about Freud's theories, about Oedipus tearing out his bleeding eyes in an extreme gesture of shame and acceptance of the fate assigned to him by the Moiras. He shook his head to rid himself of the portentous image that hovered over his brow like a ravenous crow staring into his Bolivian pupils. His hand glided down, a ship across the warm, smooth skin of Patria's belly. He continued downward towards the depths of Patria's body, she welcomed his caress—eyes half-closed, Phrygian cap off to the side on the nightstand, pink tongue moistening plump, half-open lips, letting gentle moans escape every now and then. Alfredo had closed his eyes in total surrender to his expedition, seeing everything with his fingertips, already imagining that first contact with the soft Venusian pubis that would lead to a concave seascape hidden between the warmest, moistest lips in the world. But in a shooting second—perhaps the longest—his fingers catastrophically ran aground in an unexpected geography, something different, more like a small fish in repose, a warm langoustine next to two round shapes—well, two oval-shaped testicles. Alfredo leaped out of the bed as if he'd just been electrocuted. He sprang up in the air, establishing a new world record in the high jump. He was an Olympian spring, repulsed and offended, a blinded, deceived seducer. He looked at his hands in disbelief, wanting to wash them, and then back up at Patria, searching for an explanation. Stunned, he found himself alone. He looked under the bed, in the closet, walked all around the bed, checked that his head was still where it should be. He needed a drink, a beer, a sip of wine, rum, something. But he remembered he rarely drank so he just sat still by the window and waited for morning to arrive.

He woke up with a pounding headache, each brain hemisphere turned into a pile of wet fortune cookies that were filled, not with a future prediction on a slip of paper, but with an entire roll of 16-millimetre film with a stereo track. He remembered a passage in one of the chapters of Arturo Borda's novel—novel?—*El loco* in which one of the characters plays football with a human head. That's what his head felt like. He couldn't quite remember the passage. Maybe it came from the second book of three thick volumes published by the mayor's office in La Paz to commemorate the painter's birth or death, more likely his death. After all, the painter had always been too scandalous—and alcoholic—a figure to be officially celebrated in life. To local sanctimonious critics, one day Jaime Sáenz turned his wide-brim hat around and said, "He drank simply because he felt like it." Feeling the scalpel of each word right between their eyes, his students heard his explanation and jealously guarded each word in their memory like rare coins.

Alfredo felt dry. Dry as the dry riverbeds where the only thing that runs is the wind of the Altiplano. His heart was an abandoned riverbank full of stones, the dusty river that splits the region of El Alto. Stuck in fragmented stories, hazy as if he were sitting flipping channels on the TV, zipping from one image to the next without knowing which horizon to hold on to, absolved of the task of having to imagine anything—that's how Alfredo felt. "I need to develop my characters," he said out loud, "and abandon the mimetic ground. Descriptions must transgress the boundaries of geography and reason. They must describe the words themselves." The vowels of oblivion. Without them, the void. Oblivion: the odour of mothballs, smoke and gunshots. Soiled spots on chairs no one sits on anymore. Oblivion, capital orb, endless tunnel, a bottomless hole, a well strung with the long rope of fate. A body falling inside rolled up into a ball, its foetal back plunging down in an infinite descent. The fall. The "i," the second vowel of oblivion, the most desperate one, most suitable for misery, shrieks and piss. At the end of the word, the ultimate, profound projection of the "o," the vocal one, an infinite mouth swallowing time itself. We approach the word, get close, walk up to it with our feet and our socks and the gravity of our everyday gestures. We observe it, pronounce it, devour, jot it down: "oblivion," theinfinitepossibilitiesofoblivion…oblivionoblivionoblivion oblivionoblivionoblivionoblivionoblivionoblivionobli vionoblivionoblivionoblivionoblivionoblivionobliv ionoblivionoblivionoblivionoblivionoblivionob livionoblivionoblivionoblivionoblivionoblivion oblivionoblivionoblivionoblivionoblivionoblivi onoblivionoblivionoblivionoblivionobliviono.

The infinite circle of circular doors devours us in the end. "Vowel" is the name we have given to those writerly orifices we slip on and fall into, leaping into the fragmentation of time. Time to remember now. And he remembered

hearing that first poem in kindergarten in Cochabamba—
in an old colonial house with doors so high you could
ride a horse through to enter and see all that took place
there from that bizarre height, the tiny wooden chairs,
the smell of glue, the hiss of their blunt-edged scissors,
the round tables where the budding citizens met every
day to practise the mysteries of how this world is represented and its language, one block away from the Heroínas
de la Coronilla avenue, the same year they killed Che:
"*Myshoeistootightmysockistoowarmandihaveacrazycrushonthe-
boyfromacrossthestreet.*" Little Inés, her eyes fixed on him,
swinging her arms while reciting the short composition
in civics class. The world was then a collection of faces—
teachers, parents and pupils—tenderly captivated hearing
her declamation. Inadvertently, Inés tied—inevitably and
for ever and ever—the body of diminutive Alfredo to the
holy cross of vowels and consonants that, when conjured
up, formed words that from then on would never stop
devouring him from inside with a gentle tingling sensation
that permeated him until even the very heart of his bones
had blushed. Twenty years later, Alfredo realized that in
those deep civic-minded moments he'd been shot by a first
arrow whose initial delights and subsequent mortal wounds
he would attribute to various bookish influences flowing
in all their variety and manifestations—from Rumi Ñawi's
muted passion to Larisa Fyodorovna's ardent lips, which lit
up the intense and sleepless nights of the innocuous bolshe-
vism of La Paz. It was Inés's teeth—small kernels of maize
and music—that had so deeply moved him all the down to
the very root of his hair. It was hot under the wise molle
trees in the schoolyard where preschool students had taken
out their small chairs for Civics class. He still didn't get the
exact meaning of the ritual he would experience so many

more times in his life. He also ignored its bloodier uses and consequences. But, at only five years old, Alfredo Cutipa was perfectly aware of the effervescence that overtook his school on that day and which demanded of him the most circumspect and patriotic behaviour, including properly combed hair and polished shoes. Inés, with short straight hair down to her chin, bangs lining her forehead. Inés, sowing the seeds of vowels with her maize teeth. Alfredo is in Cochabamba, in 1967, "about to enter for the first time that labyrinth of affection, where we are at once Minotaur and Theseus. We die to continue living."

In late summer of 1993, Alfredo Cutipa set out to write with renewed fervour, trying to draw with each word a trait, a feature of the face that looked him in the mirror, knowing the task was impossible.[8] Alfredo wrote knowing that the painful emergence of each word was certain proof that another word had been crushed, stabbed, bled to death in the long, dark tunnel that leads into the page after piercing through feet, chest, sex, eyes, arms and fingers. Each word the denial of another. The other one, the one that isn't here—the one that will never be here—may have been more effective, more precise, more human than this one here. He gazed for an instant at the foliage outside, the curtains quivering from the open windows in the last heat of summer, realizing that his fate was not any better than that of the curtains fluttering in the wind, or the leaves in the park clutching the branches in anticipation of a winter that was already, gently, beginning to blow on the air at dawn. Three years had passed since he had set out daily to write his long, dense novel in which he would peel, one layer at

---

8   From the point of view of another scribe and ruthless grammar stickler, the task of writing presents itself as a double impossibility: impossible to achieve and impossible to avoid.

a time, with the diligence of an ant, the intestines of his patria, which, like Goya's monstrous, insatiable Saturn at the El Prado Museum, devoured her own children, chewing on them slowly as if they were coca *acullicos*. He would thus attempt to demonstrate that the main reason for Bolivia's existence was violence. During every Montreal winter—the sky robed in the bright, light blue of a thin, giant sheet of aluminum—he hadn't stopped turning the dial on his shortwave radio. All in vain. Eventually, Bolivia started to resemble a sort of Camelot, a mythical kingdom he would never again be allowed to enter. For a long time he collected newspapers and cut out news articles; he tried to rekindle a few friendships by writing letters that were never answered; he became enraged and got drunk uttering curses in three languages and insults in two others after learning about the final results of the 1993 national elections.

In a stubborn, silent act of protest, Alfredo went to an old liquidations store on Boulevard Saint-Laurent and bought a pair of cotton-polyester socks with the colours of the Bolivian flag: red, yellow and green. He wore them as a provocative act—or at least so he thought, foolishly picturing himself bathed in the perfume of subversion and conspiracy—under a pair of ankle-length pants. He then went to every Latin-American party he learned about on posters copied and taped in corners around the immigrant neighbourhood of Côte-des-Neiges, at cafés on hedonist Rue Saint-Denis, along the cosmopolitan boulevard Saint-Laurent, on bus stops. On a Saturday evening filled with tamales and revelry, at a solidarity event for a group of persecuted aboriginal Guatemalans who had spent centuries dodging the muskets or infrared scopes of soldiers from the imperio, a woman with long black hair and eyes of grey coral thought she had recognized the political manifesto implied by his tricolour socks. She walked up to talk to him, cautiously at first, showing growing interest in him—a man who, rather than reserved, was linguistically shy. She spoke to him in French, with an accent that at times seemed from Marseille. Passionate and spontaneous, she told him about her Kurdish origins, the goals of the Kurdish cause, her experiences in France and Germany where she'd recently been working as a translator, establishing contacts and working for the PKK—Kurdistan Workers' Party—which was fighting on two fronts against oppression from Turkey and Iraq, and had recently unleashed a mighty wave of bombings against various Turkish embassies and consulates across Europe to highlight the silent complicity between Turkish and Europeans, former rivals now united in the subjugation of the Kurdish people. She didn't have a patria but dreamed of having one, while Alfredo had one but dreamed of not having it. To make matters worse, both countries, one more imaginary than the other, bore the same three colours on their flags. So Alfredo tried to make himself understood over the trumpeting salsa and merengue and the hypnotic aroma of *patacones*, tamales and *chorizos* around them. In his Cochambamba French, he explained the true meaning of his socks, the subversive effect he had intended, his vigorous, categorical rejection of his nation's flag, that infamous, insignificant, bloodstained rag that to him represented the most primitive nationalism. In that church basement in Côte-des-Neiges, the fire of his rhetoric, all the rivers of his Andean memories, his best French verb conjugations were all useless in convincing her of the real purpose of his tricolour socks. She smiled and stared at him, amused perhaps by the French accent of this man—*Alfred cette fois, ou Alfgged, avec un "r" profond et riche*—or perhaps by the crude naiveté of his explanations. For her, from the perspective of

Komala Karjeren—the Kurdish trade union movement—Alfredo's socks represented the colours of the great Kurdish patria, and the road to that promised land inexorably passed through the barrel of a rifle and the gunpowder of a bomb. Who knows if it was because they were tired of geopolitical and socio-historical reasoning, or the music that had invaded all their pores, but suddenly they both realized their bodies had begun to dialogue with each other in the oldest, most silent language on earth.

Without saying a word, at the start of a song she gestured, asking him to dance. They were playing *"La rosa negra,"* a "rhumbasalsa" by a Californian band that played guitar as if they were Gypsies, and maybe they were, since Ottmar Liebert, the name of the guitar player, sounded more Gypsy than German. But neither of them knew for sure. Instead, they thought it was a song of Central American influence whose dance style Alfredo felt compelled to explain through movement given his obvious condition of being a Latin American citizen. The guitar trembled in the speakers and the song started softly, its beat leading their feet from side to side with its jingles and drums. Gradually she became an ocean of rhythms of a sweet Oriental similarity. Her body weaved back and forth led by her hips. Alfredo felt in his bones an ache to die next to her, his Andean skin itself eyeing her eagerly. He felt as if his senses had just crossed forty arduous years of chaste, solitary deserts. His pulse discovered a latent, expectant force, a hidden sensuality that through her insinuated the power of all the oceans. Standing close to her he thought of the destruction and decadence caused by time passing, the bombs and gunshots fed by faith, and the hearts that so would have loved the colour of the dawn. He thought of rusted clocks and the silent decay of yellowing letters accumulated over the years. He thought in that instant that all his contact with humanity, with the other, was reduced to that fleeting moment when you touch another person capable of all the affections available at the tip of their fingers, about to cross the threshold of their senses. He quietly sent endless blessings to the breath, sweat and words of the bards of old who thousands of years ago urged in word and deed to seize the present moment with both hands, both eyes, both mouths, both hearts and deeply breathe in life's fragrance. For an instant, spinning around, standing in that epicentre surrounded by music, arms, spices, tones, accents and sayings of the Latin American tongue, Alfredo felt himself gradually descend to the faraway South: idealized, dusty, sentimental and terribly poor. "Her arms inhabited my back and my hand descended to the swaying port of her waist. Music invaded her eyes, made waves in her hair. For an instant I was fast and moved deftly on my feet, trying to be a seasoned Latin American..." he would write later, knowing that perhaps this way, thanks to the written word, she would remain by his side forever. The fervour of the guitars subsided and a slow cascade of melodies fell. They stopped spinning and their bodies remained close, holding on, and decided to stay together forever.

They took a cab together at the end of the party. The Haitian driver welcomed them with blasting kompa music, his shoulders dancing as he drove his metal ship around Montreal at dawn. Moments later, trying hard to drive away the intrusion of an old, terrible dream, Alfredo turned off the light and plunged into a blissful sea of kisses. He leaned against his bedroom wall and launched his hands, sails in the wind, two boats setting out on a voyage around the world to cross the farthest, most mysterious straits. Smooth, resplendent breasts. Soft hips. A curious navel, forever admiring itself in another. The lower his hand went, the slower his journey became, the more cautious his touch, until he finally reached—eager and relieved—the Ithaca every Ulysses dreams of. His arrival turned the night into a dazzling, erotic ocean of hymens and seashells. Alfredo opened his eyes and with trumpeting fanfare he flamboyantly unfurled his sex, which to her seemed sufficient, if not particularly extraordinary. The next morning he would learn that the woman—who had held him and showered him with love and bites, pushed him off the side of a cliff, and abandoned him in the centre of a now-dead volcano—was gone and had left a brief note on the table: *Mon Alfredo: Merci pour tout ton amour. Il est 7 heures du matin et je dois te quitter. Je t'aime bien, mon gauchiste-caviar. À bientôt. Bolivia.*[9]

"No! What the...? This can't be! For god's sake! A Kurdish woman named Bolivia... Who the hell would give that name to a woman born in Sulaymaniyah?"

Alfredo buttoned up his shirt, still shocked by his discovery and fatigued in that peculiar way you feel after a long night in bed with a woman. He noticed his subversive tricolour socks had disappeared. He knelt down to look under the bed for the umpteenth time, somewhat surprised by the odd occurrence.

Two days later, Alfredo decided to look for Bolivia all over the island of Montreal. He returned to the quiet church basement where he'd met her. He spied from the doors at any Latin American fiesta that popped up. He visited Turkish and Lebanese spice stores. Six months later, his search hadn't yielded any favourable results. He visited hostels, university dorms and old rooming

9   "My Alfredo: Thank you for your love. It's 7 o'clock in the morning and I have to leave you. I like you a lot, my caviar leftist. See you soon, Bolivia."

house buildings. He crossed the patinated iron bridges that lead to Longueil and Laval, returned to his room exhausted and dismayed. He wished he could remember her perfume, retain even a trace of her, but he remembered nothing—that night, the only thing he could sense in the air, on the Kurdish woman's skin, was the scent of words, that airplane smell, the air suitcases retain when they return from a remote place. One afternoon in those days of endless searching, Alfredo happened upon the Kurdish social club two blocks from Montreal's Jean Talon Market. It was both a café and a store of sorts, one of those places where somewhat stolid men with nostalgic eyes and proud moustaches gathered around the tables, conversing quietly while drinking coffee or playing chess or reading newspapers whose worn pages showed the transit of thousands of eyes and fingertips—news that may have been as fresh as dried figs, written in a language whose architecture of lines resembled the inscriptions found on ancient mosques. Alfredo stepped inside. He noticed no one wore tricolour socks there. At the counter, a display of banners, t-shirts and even porcelain cups with the three colours of the Bolivian flag—that is, the Kurdish flag. They were focused as they smoked, some with their hands in their pockets, others with *komboloi* beads sliding slowly through their fingers one after the other, listening attentively as Alfredo described the Kurdish woman who'd recently arrived in Montreal after spending time in France and Germany, and he'd had the pleasure to meet at a solidarity gathering. Alfredo explained all of this to the Kurds at the joint, speaking English at times, at times in French, but always avoiding specific intimate details, naturally. While explaining he came from a country whose flag was the same as Kurdistan, the country they so yearned for, he noticed they were now beginning to exchange short questioning phrases, their looks hesitant and suspicious, maybe thinking he was a spy.

Six months after he'd written, "No! What the...? This can't be! For god's sake! A Kurdish woman named Bolivia... Who the hell would give that name to a woman born in Sulaymaniyah?" Alfredo was sitting at his kitchen table in his small Villeray apartment, trying in vain, again, to write, hoping the exercise would finally take that thorn of *Puya raimondi* that pierced his head from ear to ear, a sensation that had become a flooding feeling of Bolivianity. Winter was being merciful despite the naked outlines of the trees on the street. Why should I feel Bolivian? Why not feel Garcilasian, and say you were born in a place called "Los heraldos negros"? The name even sounds like a place where luscious oaks grow and give good shade. But no. Alfredo Cutipa—whose right ring finger and little finger had almost been bitten off by a monkey at the zoo on the other side of the Rocha River on a remote childhood afternoon—felt irrationally, earthily Bolivian.

Cardán, I'm sure you remember that night, and correct me if I'm wrong, cross out this line, tear up this page, grab a new one and write down what you think really happened. I'm telling you about the night Boxeador died, when we found pieces of his skull embedded in the wooden beams that held up the roof in guard post number eleven—or was it sixteen?—in that vast space at the El Alto Air Base, and we found at our feet brain mass spread in all directions of the highlands, globs of white and greyish gelatinous matter running down the adobe walls, their tiny veins still pulsating. Do you remember? Remember, because the dead only die for real when no one can remember them anymore. Correct me if I'm wrong, Cardán *hermano*, because I don't even know if I remember these things. These days people don't like to remember. People say memory is for old people—when it's passive—or they'll say you're being seditious and dissatisfied if you want to know the how and why of every story. Maybe I remember because it's a lie that the dead are asleep. It's a lie they are only dust. The worms may have feasted on their bodies, hands, tongues and eyes, and there may be no heaven or hell beyond the infinity of those tireless microscopic jaws, but their images remain, their voices remain inside of us. There are those who insist in making us believe everything that happens, life and death, is all due to divine will. That all the misery and atrocities in this life will be rewarded after death with gentle geographies, celestial clouds of milk and manna. They say all of this because they have candles to sell, alms to hand out, believers to domesticate and miseries to justify. Or perhaps it's because the dead are more rebellious than anyone else. There's nothing you can do to them. You can't arrest them, beat them or exile them, and they live and come near us with their restlessness, and they leave whenever they please, they go up and down, go from night to day, from sleep to wakefulness, and sometimes they whisper stories in our ear while we sleep, without us noticing that their bones become the roots that guide our very steps, nimble bones moving underground the way a pianist's fingers would accompany us, guide us until the moment comes when we, too, will whisper our last words before plunging into the same silence with our mouth full of dirt. Then, with that same dirt filling our eye sockets, kneecaps and ribcages, we will speak sweetly with the living, telling them about the things we've seen and how the double edge of dust and oblivion is killing us little by little. I don't know who ended up picking up the bloody body of that soldier of the second company of Air Base fusiliers. I don't even know if they took what was left of him in a stretcher. I don't remember if his body exhaled a something, a soul, as it was lifted. I don't know if his body was rigid and resisting death, or was a flaccid empty costume discarded on the floor after a sad party. I knew Boxeador had come to the city from somewhere in the Altiplano, stubbornly set on enduring one year in the Army. Just like him, every year hundreds, thousands of indigenous youth left the deepest regions of the Andean lands and headed to the barracks to meet the violent rite of passage. They arrived at the doors in silence. They arrived after days of anticipation. They spent their hours and their nights waiting for the regiment doors to open—artillery, motorized cavalry, infantry—waiting for their sergeants to take their name and last name, to examine their teeth, waiting for the army physicians to mark their chests with odd numbers written in iodine on their skin, waiting for the armed doctors to spread their butt cheeks to check for haemorrhoids. There were always extras—too many boys begging in Aymara, "Let me join up, sergeant, don't be mean, I don't have enough money for the bus back to my community. I can't go back until I'm a veteran." The first month of military service, Boxeador was an extra, wasn't needed in the company and in the battalion. But he insisted in staying and began as a supernumerary. He made it work, slept on the cement floor with no mattress and only one blanket, he was stubborn against the cold and lack of food, and he endured every single insult and humiliation, for better or for worse. Supernumeraries like him didn't have access to a sleeping cot, supplies or anything else. But he'd decided to stay no matter what and endure anything that came his way.

On his first day off, the first break for conscripts to return to old civilian life, Boxeador finally managed to secure a sleeping cot for himself. This, because many of the new recruits never returned to the barracks, possessed by the frenzy of prisoners who have just been released, burdened by the language, hygiene, elegant manners and finesse of Bolivia's military world. It was mostly those lucky enough to have family in La Paz who could free themselves from having to return to the filthy military barracks. City dwellers were spared having to step back into reeking, tattered uniforms inherited from other bodies and miseries. The families of those who ignored the motherland's call would later take care of bribing the appropriate military authorities and obtain the military service card that opened doors to higher education, employment and the right to vote. Others, like Boxeador, whose Native families lacked the necessary funds and language, who'd come from lost places on the republic's map, had to stick it out because they couldn't show their face in their hometowns, where many of their relatives, with an absurd dose of pride, were already spreading the news that their sons were serving the nation to become real men—able to get drunk, build a hut and choose a woman they would hit every once in a while following the military style they'd learned. The sacred vulture perched on the oval in the national coat of arms presaged the fundamental notions of the Bolivian nation. God, patria, home. Perhaps Boxeador thought that's what it meant to be a Bolivian Native or mestizo: to be capable of absolute stoicism and resistance, capable of being a heroic wall that could stop the machinegun fire of the enemy, be they *rotos*, *pilas* or Red, and do anything to serve the great Bolivian Patria. To embody the myth of the bronze race, that which dies at the base of the cannon, that which endures everything.

But that bronze race doesn't exist, it never existed because behind that imaginary Andean stoicism there is nothing but infinite, exhausted resignation, even greater than Illimani itself. The bronze race was invented to legitimize violence: the Andean can endure anything, suffer through anything. Ponguito who never complains. Little miner who thinks he'll be rewarded in heaven after singing about his sombre mineshaft days and tragic nights. Sardine-eating little worker. Little builder made of bread, banana and papaya. *Indiecito, campesino buenagente.* Little thief with no bad intentions. He's just drunk, leave him alone. He'll take it, he'll just take it because a good Bolivian, because he's made of bronze. Metal doesn't talk or suffer or feel, and it bends only in the fire. Bronze race for the Palacio Quemado condors to defecate on.

They put him in a makeshift casket bought last-minute in the slums of El Alto. It wasn't very solid—rather rustic with a light coat of varnish with bare spots in the wood. I don't know if it was Sergeant Walter Rubin de Celis, Non-Commissioned Officer Juan Barrón Huet, Lieutenant Torres or first battalion commander Major Trifón Echalar Miranda who gave the order to buy two 25-litre cans of 100-proof Caimán-brand liquor so they could prepare *té con té* for the wake. It was almost midnight and the quarters where soldiers in other companies slept—unaware of what had happened—were still quiet, barely lit by the dim yellow lamps that edged the battalion's square. One week earlier, the soldiers had limed the walls of the dorms. The off-white greyish walls were pale and ghostly like a screen in the ruins of an abandoned movie theatre. Every so often, steps would echo through the space, grumbling faraway voices repeating the mechanical nightly ritual of "Stopwhosthere!", soldiers who went from post to post in the cold darkness of the

Altiplano, rifle on their shoulder. Soldiers on watch at their adobe, calamine and straw quarters would return the tired watchword selected for the night followed by the recited formula: "Guardpostnumberelevennothingtoreport." That night our company was the only one busy with wake arrangements. At his own or someone else's hand, Boxeador had died fulfilling his duty, in full service to the patria, blocking the enemy—whoever they were—at the northeast end of the military base. Death came disguised in 7.62 calibre when it blasted his brown Andean body and sank its fangs of smoke, gunpowder and metal into his skull. It was cold in the early dawn hours. The Altiplano wind was blowing, lifting small swirls of paper, plastic bags and garbage in the garrison yard. Our superiors ordered us to change out of our daily fatigues—old, mended rough wool—and don a newer cotton-polyester formal uniform and light cap. We were posted as the honour guard at each cardinal point of the casket, in the centre of the improvised reposing room in the officers' casino. We all took shifts watching the body of the dead soldier until it was time to bury him at the General Cemetery. Cardán, do you remember when we walked into the room where the body was and there were already four soldiers from our company standing at each corner of the casket, their faces sullen, sad and absent? A few soldiers decided to close the coffin to avoid looking straight at the corpse, to evade the intense gaze of his single eye, the only thing left on Boxeador's face. The sergeant on duty that week, in charge of the eighty-one soldiers in company B, ordered all personnel to be present equipped with their tin mugs. Every so often, two soldiers filled the mugs to the brim with a potent mix of liquor and *agua de sultana* in the last instants of martial pain with the mangled soldadito boliviano. Officers from other companies in attendance sat on one side of the officers' casino, some half asleep, some sipping the coarse *té con té*, admiring within their inner jurisdiction the stoicism required for someone to put the barrel of a rifle under his chin and pull the trigger. Three shots had come out of Boxeador's automatic rifle. The first pierced the visor of his kepi and launched it across the room—we later found it curled up in a corner of the guard post. The second bullet sliced open his lips, eyebrow and forehead as if he'd been hit with a sabre or a bayonet, tearing off one of his nostrils as well. The third bullet hit his left malar bone causing a massive earthquake in his facial nerves and muscles. The power of the shot tore through all tissue in its path like a battering ram, blowing up his eyeball, inferior cranial wall, part of his frontal bone, parietal bone and the entire side of his skull. His brain burst and splattered pieces of brain mass everywhere and embedded bone splinters in the walls and wooden beams. Around 2:00 AM the officers went to sleep, bored by a death that had failed to be epic. We simple soldiers stayed behind with Boxeador's body. Perhaps because for many it was our first time drinking such a cruel alcoholic mix, or because our empty stomachs were being eaten away by the liquor, or perhaps because the spectacle of death before us was terrifying and hypnotizing, suddenly some of the mourners began to stumble around. Some dozed off and fell off their chairs, woke up frightened upon finding themselves in a place they didn't recognize and quietly slipped away to their dorms. The soldiers' faces began to lose their shape, became stretched and distorted. Against the military casino's walls, their faces turned the bitter yellow-green of the walls in that painting at the Guggenheim showing gaunt soldiers in a shower. Silhouettes softened as dawn approached. Noises reached us taking long, slow steps. Some of the soldiers looked like sleepy children wandering through the casino hall, their faces flooded with guilt and regret as if their presence at the station, at the funeral, was somehow a betrayal to their families. A voice began to hum a Native song, perhaps a *yaraví*, while the rifles started walking around on their own and mingling with the chairs, pouring *té con té* into their thin barrels whose necks and long beaks stretched out like a flock of black storks drinking out of tin mugs. Some soldiers held their weapons tenderly, or yelled at them, or whispered to them calling them their *cholas*, their sweethearts, twisting their belt around their arms, giving them slow sips or sprinkling them with alcohol in a sort of baptism—a mythical *challa*. "*Estoy challando a mi chola,*" they explained with a grimace and a twang in their voice. They would laugh and repeat the Carnival Tuesday ritual over and over. Then either the dead soldier got up, only a few shreds of charred lips on his face, or the casket fell on the ground when someone bumped into it and the body rolled out of the casket like a doll. A few solicitous soldiers approached him, talking to him in Aymara and Spanish, grabbing him by the arms. They propped him up on a chair against the wall. Boxeador sat and leaned what was left of his head on one of his shoulders. He was drunk, too. Someone put a mug of *té con té* in his bruised hands. We could see he wasn't dead. He was with us, or we were with him, and instead of blood his flesh and exposed bone were oozing a yellowish fluid, like blood mixed with sugarcane juice, and it became lodged in our throats and mixed with the sweet taste of liquor in the *té con té* we were drinking. That was the scent of our own baptism, the mark, the sign of a ritual that would never leave us. Death welcomed us joyfully in her domains, inebriated us, seduced us and made us laugh showing us what she was capable of. Somehow that night ripped something out from deep inside our bones. We lost something and were ever since then incomplete, fragmented. Some soldiers cried in a corner watching Boxeador's incomplete, disfigured face. Another cried and didn't notice himself wetting his pants. We were floating in the air. At one point we walked up to Boxeador and formed a semicircle around him, asked him why he'd died, if he'd been killed, what death was like. He looked at us with his one good eye, an island of light in a bloody, black-and-blue face and responded by sweating tiny beads of blood that struggled not to clot and dry up. He tried to have a drink but couldn't move his lips. Someone dipped a handkerchief in *té con té* and put it to his lips. Slowly Boxeador savoured that last sip with what was left of his mouth. We said goodbye, told him to take care of himself. We promised we would always remember him and hugged him as if he'd just won the most important boxing match in Bolivia's history. Moved by all the attention he was receiving, as if we'd all forgotten we were *indios*, mestizos, *indios* again and sometimes white coming together to be close to him, he decided to spare us further pain. He wobbled and stood up slowly. He felt his way across the short distance between his chair and the casket, which was now back on top of two tripods in the middle of the room. He climbed into his coffin as delicately as one would climb onto a *totora* raft swaying in the middle of Lake Titicaca, sat down and arranged himself inside his wooden boat and looked at us one more time. He wanted to say something but he no longer had a voice, so with a small movement of his hand he lay back down in his coffin. He then became still forever. By then, sleep had slowed down our breathing, and fatigue yawned heavily on our eyelids. Some of us stepped outside and headed to our sleeping quarters—the stars above spiralled in the still dawn sky like eyes around a faint eddy reflecting in our pupils. I managed to drag my body all the way to the edge of my cot. Someone cried out in the distance, *"Buenas noches, Boxeador."* Another voice responded, *"Güenas."*

January of 1994 brought days in which Alfredo could see in the open space of his imagination words flying high in the distance—magnificent migratory birds he'd never be able to see up close, never be able to make them say anything on the silent horizon of every page. All he could do was take refuge again in the black waters of the river that splits past from present, ruthlessly condemned to be the boatman between two shores that would never meet, carrying dead bodies from all the deaths he'd had to die. In 1980, Alfredo had died twice, a hundred times, a thousand times, and since then—who knows if for a long time before—he hadn't stopped dying steadily and relentlessly, and yet every morning he'd hold himself up standing before his piles of paper, invigorated and full of words—first words, last words, the ones no one would ever hear, brought by the imaginary *huayra* and harmattan air streams, having crossed gullies, cordilleras and deserts, carrying to his ears and hands the whispers, sighs and voices born in some street, city or region he would never know. Clutching his pen, he would write down the taut urgency of desires—those that come first, those that come last, in various tongues and scripts. Alfredo's pages were inhabited by all the desires of the world, filled with words that mingled with threads of memory and the swollen currents that rushed down the streets and tore up the urban bedrock of La Paz in February.

The first time he died, he'd been warned in a dream he hadn't known how to decipher. In the dream, Amelia—a young woman with long hair and fine lips—spoke to him through fragmented images and large gestures from the other side of a thick clear wall, as if she were under an old bell jar, the kind used in old houses to store heirloom antique clocks and protect their delicate gearbox from the dust. At her gesturing, he woke up drenched in sweat in the quiet dorm he shared with ninety other teenaged soldiers enrolled in compulsory military service under threat of imprisonment, imposed by the ever-malleable national laws. He was sleeping, and in his dream he was waking up inside another dream, a sheltered microscopic fossil in the intricate strata of his memory. A sleeping soldier was muttering incomprehensibly at the back of the large dorm, somewhere in the dark forest of four-level loaded bunk beds. Slightly more awake now, he looked up in the half-light and saw a boy in the silence of the Andean night. He was sitting on wooden boxes near the window, looking over the vast cradle of the sleeping city and watching the stars spin above the Ceja de El Alto. Alfredo got up quietly. His boots untied and his dreamed face of Amelia still fresh in his retina, he crept through the dorm's big metal gate out to the wide cement-and-stone yard. He scurried with his back against the wall, his ear sharp to evade the officers doing military rounds, who could capture and punish his alleged escape by putting him behind bars for weeks in the adobe and rammed-earth guardroom. It was March and the night air chilled his eyelids when he stepped out to the main yard of the Air Force Security and Defence Unit. He stopped to tie his bootlaces and felt the pungent smell of uric acid. The pale light of the night revealed hundreds of damp snaking tracks, a wide and fetid filigree covering the ground. Every night at bedtime, to encourage the purest patriotic sentiment in the uniformed mass, army officers ordered thousands of conscripts to repeat an innocent war cry: "Viva Bolivia! Death to Chile! Aaaah!" The scream required special attention—in more than a few occasions hundreds of soldiers had been severely punished for failing to produce it adequately. It wasn't meant to convey defeat or sound like someone being wounded. In Bolivia's dense military tradition, the goal was to accompany the bayonet in its mortal drive into the enemy's body. After repeating the fierce phrase, sometimes framed in laughter, the little Bolivian soldiers would joke around on their way to their dorms, emptying their bladders as they walked and sang in chaotic military formation, avoiding their comrades' boots to prevent the potential resulting insults and fistfights, weaving night after night an endless carpet of micturations. Now the urine snakes slept quietly in the centre yard, vanishing slowly under patches lit by weak spotlights that fought in vain against the darkness. He moved slowly with his back against the wall, a cautious fox seeking invisibility in the cover of darkness. He crossed the yard and reached the back of the troop dorms—he could see the hangars of sleeping rheumatic T-33 aircraft, left over from the Korean War, ancient military donations and source of boundless pride for the thantosa Bolivian aviation. He crossed the road that stood between the night and Amelia's voice and reached the only telephone available to the almost eight hundred soldiers in his battalion. There was no one there. A good sign. He looked up at the stars, trying to guess the time, imagining his beautiful Amelia's surprise upon receiving his call. He picked up the receiver, searched in his pocket for a coin, inserted it in the slot and entered her number in the slow rotary dial.

For years, that name—Amelia—even before recalling her figure or her face, had had enough power to keep him awake entire nights. In bed, eyes open or closed, he restlessly reconstructed in his memory the city corners he'd walked through every time he went to see her. Alfredo remembered every house, every window and every dog bark along the way. He'd actually gone to see her only once, but in his imagination there were many—enough to feed night after sleepless night. Perhaps she had invited him over for tea or to listen to music; or he had invented some unlikely reason to go to her house in Miraflores, near Plaza Germán Bush, an enormous square that hosted the annual flamboyant military parades to honour the national flag. He arrived at the red metal door, looked at the blue walls, then up at the pine branches over the roof tiles that capped the wall around the house. He coughed nervously before ringing the bell. He could recall the colour of her skin, her beaming eyes, her delicate knuckles, her measured voice, her teeth, the blouse she was wearing that afternoon, the tenderness in her arms, her lips, her entire being. He filled his chest at the closed door and rang the bell. He waited, and waited, and waited. A pair of eyes scrutinized him at length through a crack, judging whether he was drunk or armed, and finally, as the door opened, Alfredo heard a familiar song. Hanging in the air over cigarette smoke and people's sweat, a song by a fiercely anti-Castro singer, a beautiful and maternal *gusana*, a political term used to refer to enemies of the Cuban revolution—as his Chilean friends and devoted militants of the party of socialist nostalgia had carefully explained to him one afternoon over coffee, empanadas and a *barros luco* sandwich at Montreal's El Refugio bakery. The song, "*Mi Tierra*," was playing on a record as the barflies danced with admirable dedication, sweating and admiring their own reflections in the mirror that lined the wall along the dance floor. In a double rise and fall, the dancers' bodies turned and got drunk on music from a mythical collective patria. *"La gente toma aguardiente porque es valiente,"*[10] a few Central Americans sang with their shirts unbuttoned—happy, sweaty Sancho Panzas. They danced in a loud unison and were finally swallowed into the unstoppable waves of salsas and merengues that followed at an impossible volume, a sort of high mass full of rituals and contortions that only the initiated understood and could execute thanks to the vigour of their hips and shoulders. Watching the clamour around his table, Alfredo wrote in his small notebook about the moment he'd knocked at Amelia's door at her old house in La Paz. He was absolutely convinced his descriptions could never recreate the buzzing beat that penetrated the tables and his kidneys, made his glass vibrate, his pores flood and his underarms quiver while he just sat there trying to define and find meaning in his constant going back in time, confused and not knowing whether he was in the past—standing by a telephone at the El Alto garrison about to call Amelia, or reminiscing about the only day he'd visited her in Miraflores—or in a future point in the story and was now folklorizing himself listening to Gloria Estefan in some bar in Montreal, or if he was alone at last with pen and paper, anywhere in the world at any time, witnessing the increasing fragmentation of his mind. Does time actually pass or is it a continuous simultaneity in which past, present and future end up tangled up in a circular chaos? Four women walked into the bar with a man whose cunning eyes began to scan the place for a table for his entourage. One of the women gathered and put her hair back into a neat bun. Alfredo suddenly remembered a story about

---

10   "People drink firewater because they're brave."

a passionate couple that walks into a café where people reeking of loneliness come hoping to find someone to say good morning to or hold during long winter nights. They sit and pretend to read a newspaper, sneak spying looks at each other guessing who is the unhappiest loner among them, who has no chance at all. A couple arrives—impetuous kisses, excited hands, beaming eyes—and the timid souls end up biting their lips, sipping unsweetened solitude from their cups between deep bitter sighs, knowing the happiness they were witnessing would forever refuse them. Alfredo tried to convince himself of his good and non-alcoholic reasons for being at the noisy bar. His theory was that, in the midst of that brutal chaos of people, music, smoke, noise, screams, lights, fistfights, and rum, he could achieve such complete inner silence that words emerged without effort. A word-hunting trick. The confusion in the space allowed words to emerge as trusting and innocent as groundhogs at the end of the winter, and find themselves trapped on a piece of paper. His trap—like the long, thin tongue of an anteater—had captured many words. How many? Hundreds, thousands, ten million words per day. He noticed he was almost out of rum, which had failed to melt the heart of the massive block of awkward bashfulness that remained lodged inside him and gave no indication of wanting to leave. He'd need to order another rum before he could launch into the centre of the dance floor, a discombobulated hybrid—quixotic windmill and headless chicken in euphoric rapture—able to defeat all distance, absence and nostalgia. Three glasses later he was still sitting there, unable to convince his feet to move while his stubborn hands worked on building a bridge of words that—he presumed—would enable him to travel across one more night. He only came to the place to drink a little rum, pretend he was in Havana or Barranquilla, La Paz, Toronto, Motril or Cochabamba, and try to tempt words to come out, to go on a date with him, who waited for them devotedly holding a bouquet of paper-and-charcoal flowers.

He recognized a few faces, met familiar eyes. When he finally managed to dance, it was so pathetic everyone around him ended up fleeing the dance floor. At least, he reflected afterwards, a charitable soul had agreed to dance with him. In the midst of his rhythmical efforts, a storm of deep, heavy sound drops began to fall, the notes, synthesizers and mechanical construction of a bad song in English—"Baby, don't hurt me... no more..." The singer's voice scribbled sadly in the air and the couples broke up and made their way back to their tables in the dim Latin club.

"Are you all right?" Amelia's voice asked, reaching across the waters of a long-gone trip to Urmiri. Alfredo turned around feigning calm, barely concealing his shock at the apparition, a dusty echo in the middle of a Montreal bar. He answered with a nod. They didn't say a word. He kept his gaze soft, avoiding looking straight at Amelia so that her image and voice wouldn't vanish into the cigarette smoke. The beat of the music that threatened to rupture his eardrums was shaking the ashtray one millimetre at a time towards the edge of the table. A woman at a nearby table lit a match and in the flame's glow Amelia's features and voice vanished for an instant. Farther out in the centre of the night, two women had joined in a slow dance, one tongue finding the other, their hips moving back and forth to the beat as they felt and caressed each other. "Would you like to dance?" Alfredo asked the visitor.

"You know I can't," Amelia replied in a low voice, "but I can tell you when you're going to die."

"I don't want to know," he mumbled. "Why did you come here with those funeral words?"

"No, no, I'm not kidding, Alfredo! Just the opposite. You have no idea how much I would have liked to know exactly which day I was going to die. That way I would have been able to come closer to you and prepared myself for this fragility. I could have reciprocated some of your long, quiet devotion. I could have gone to the station that night to find you and say you'd never see me again, to say goodbye and tell you not to waste your time calling me because it was too late for both of us. That way they wouldn't have beaten you so hard for trying to make a call that was never answered. Because when they were beating you, Alfredo, I was fading away, my body died little by little with every single blow. You've been waiting for me for how long, ten, fifteen years?"

"Sixteen years, Amelia, sixteen."

"How was I supposed to know you'd written all those pages you used to read for me when you came to visit? That you'd created and written them just for me? You never explained. After you let me read them, you'd only say you'd found an interesting book somewhere, or a notebook with no name or address in the back of a bus, stuff like that. You know how much you lie."

"That's not true. I've never written anything about you before tonight."

"You're such a bad liar, Alfredo. Will you ever change?"

He lied to her. How could he tell her he'd always been looking for her, that all he could do to try to remember her was to write, try to build a house of words, a book, a space where he'd always be able to find her after all those years, free from death, free from forgetting and silence?

"You weren't really looking for me, Alfredo. You're fine just waiting for me from this side of reality. If you were really looking for me, you would have done something else. You would have come back and looked for me."

He didn't know what to say. And she could tell. There was no point hiding the flow of his thoughts. Amelia could sense every image and idea in Alfredo's mind as if she lived in the centre of his imagination, as if his thoughts, while he sat there in a bar in Montreal, were as sharp as hearing someone scream in the middle of a nave in a colonial church. She continued, "Can't you see I've also been waiting for you in my own way? Keeping you company, watching the way you love, the way you hate, watching you even while you looked for me in other women?"

"Tell me, Amelia, what good is it loving a ghost? Someone who's not there anymore, who's just a memory, a dead woman who left without saying a word, without even saying if she ever loved me or not?"

"You're right, Alfredo. I don't have an answer for you. But you're here, and you keep looking for me, talking to me, writing to me…"

It was true. He'd continued to look for her even though he knew it was pointless, and impossible. He downed the rest of the lukewarm rum in his glass and ordered a beer—it was Saint-Jean-Baptiste Day in Montreal, a humid summer night, so distant, so different from cold June nights in the Andean winter. The last time he saw her was on a night like that. They were standing near one of thousands of festive bonfires, flowers of light that brightened the nocturnal cradle of La Paz and cast small sparkles on her long dark hair. Wanting to find her now was like trying to write a novel he'd never be able to finish. All he could manage to write in his notebooks was his own doubts, this anguish of those who study the traces of Death, those who search for the roots of their own voice. Now, back in this space for dance and pagan rituals, a woman bloomed into a cumbia—her hips and long hair swaying, her feet moving to the beat. In a final gesture, a reckless seducer waved the banners of his hands towards the woman's breasts, received in return a majestic smack across the face. The ardent *latinillo* walked off with his tail between his legs, away from the woman, who remained in possession of the cumbia, of the space and of herself.

He looked around for Amelia so they could keep talking, but she'd vanished. "Even dead people leave me," he thought to himself. All he had left were the blind workers of his words—ants, unconcerned by any diegetic intentions.

"What good is it to love a dead woman?" Amelia's voice asked out of nowhere, a sudden whisper in his ear. He looked up from his notebook but couldn't see her. She was invisible and ethereal, only a whispering voice that would keep him company, then vanish. For an instant he thought he recognized her sitting at a table. Yes, Amelia was there, at the other end of the nightclub—her expression was serene, fine fingers interlaced under her chin, eyes fixed on him, the slightest smile drawn on her face. The woman sitting next to her turned around to look at Alfredo. As soon as his pupils touched her gaze, she averted her eyes and looked towards the other end of the bar. The last he saw of Amelia was her hand waving affectionately while she mouthed a quiet *"Chao."* Then her shape and her long, black shiny hair began to vanish little by little, penetrating, inhabiting, merging with the shape, body and features of the woman sitting beside her, who right then looked at Alfredo again, this time straight at him, looking to make eye contact. The eyes of a woman of this world dropped their anchors into the figure of the confused Andean man. He muttered something at the vision—perhaps a "*qué jodida la cosa, che*" or "*chao, Amelia*"—and, as if beckoned by a revelation, he ascended into the ether of the night, driven by the blind logic of the ancestral dancer in his blood. He looked one last time at the now empty spot where Amelia had been sitting and talking to him and, feeling intensely Latin, he leapt head first into the dance floor with the unknown woman who was walking towards him. His joints didn't loosen up. His Andean hips failed to sway. But she—perhaps born from ancient, fertile Irish humus on Canadian land—surrounded him with the cadence of her arms, offered him the bread of her hair, water from her brow, made the earth turn under his feet to allow his ankles and the planets to rotate. The drums played, the rum sang from the ice, and she became pure in her spinning, a waterfall in the night, joyous in her half turn, as if her hips had suddenly learned to speak, testing the limits and possibilities of a body dancing in the night, performing the most remote, most sacred exercise in human memory. She moved closer, leaned rhythmical and vertebral, and turned, a moist river of music. "I'd rather gaze at your arms in flight, how the black wheat fields spin before my eyes, your moist brow upon my shoulder. Water in your waist, water in your knees, and the moons of your chest point with their hidden light at the path that leads to the heart of the drums and the night."

After dancing and duly conveying his appreciation to the woman, back in his rum-and-glass island refuge, a man looks out on this sea of steps and songs, lumber and certainty, watches a woman seed a cumbia with her fingers, feet and hips. Music has devoured the faces and identities. You can't see her anymore but you know Amelia is here, spinning around you in the air, to the beat of the drums and maracas in the dome of this heart, beckoning your pupils to imagine the past, inventing this hand whose only territory is now a waist and some music.

No one picked up the phone. It rang and rang. No one. No one. Alfredo waited in vain for someone to answer and take him from that phone at the Air Base to Amelia's mouth, to the full moon of her voice lighting up the night inside his chest. But a stealth serpent emerged from a well of wrath—a low-ranking officer on duty appeared beside him. Thirty years later, Alfredo would think to himself the officer had been without a doubt the kind that believed in monument heroes, in the martial glory shining in Charles Dumoulin's eyes, in blazing cavalry attacks where ancient combat fencing is still used for a rifle barrel to block a sabre blow from a moustached hussar on horseback—his splendid replica covered in dust and blood sleeps eternal and agitated behind glass at Les Invalides. But the officer knew none of this. His personal taste was dissatisfied with the size of the golden lead stars on his epaulettes, small scatological decorations—like the pigeon droppings on Plaza Murillo's heroic monuments—that signalled the supreme condition of lieutenant that he had achieved. *"Ah! Mono! Monito...* At my command! Atten-HUT! Half left, FACE!"* ordered the Bolivian Ethereal Farce officer, who had resigned himself to being an army lieutenant, unable to withstand height vertigo and the unsteady flight of the T-33s that had miraculously survived the fire of North Korean anti-aircraft batteries. "So the little monkey's chatting with his *chola! Ah mono, youdumbasslittlemonkey...*" In his punishment position, Alfredo knew he couldn't even look towards the part of the city where even the cobblestones loved the echo of Amelia's steps. The order was that severe. His obedience was that stupid. The officer grabbed the receiver and waited for someone to pick up. It was his practice to use the soldiers' women. He would cheat them into bringing them to the station—"You'll only get liberty if your girlfriend comes to visit you, but you'll go out on your own, she stays with me." He would break the soldiers by beating and smearing feces on them, force them bring their girlfriends to the station, introduce them to him freshly showered, perfumed and full of trust and affection. And devoted, they would come to see their men, their little bronze soldiers, bringing them treats, smokes, letters and kisses, unaware of the superiors' lurid orders, the wooden boards splintering on the backs and buttocks of those who refused to comply. More than a few girlfriends, friends and sisters had ended up with blood running down their legs following a violent, heroic military assault against the red enemy's trenches in the name of the highest interests of the Motherland. Perhaps that's why Boxeador's brains ended up scattered on the beaten earth floors inside a guard post—lost in an Altiplano that slowly lost ground to the city and its noises, which slowly swallowed up the wind that whistled in the rough grass. The officer scratched his crotch. He waited anxiously with the receiver stuck to his ear, growing impatient while waiting, like Alfredo, for someone to answer. The soldier in his punishment position now wished with all his heart for no one to pick up at Amelia's house. The officer started to swear and yell at the mute receiver. "Pickupthefuckingphonerightnow!" unaware that Amelia was slowly losing consciousness at the other end of the line. Collapsed on the floor, a stroke was quickly draining her last lucid moments. Her breath slowly faded away while a phone rang relentlessly in the next room. "Yourejustfuckingwithme, youmonkeypieceofshit!" the officer threatened him. He slammed the phone down and, out of the dark, sucker-punched Alfredo, who crumpled to the ground, his mouth open, his eyes loaded with constellations. Private Alfredo Cutipa, second company in the air defence battalion, fell, covered in dust and pleased with the pain of knowing no one had picked up the phone, knowing that Amelia was free from the viscous voice, the feverish hands, the greyish fingers and fingernails of the Bolivian army man who was kicking him into the ground.

That 1st day of January 1995, he arrived on the island of Montreal on a snow sled pulled by penguins. He was stealth, like the secrets he was struggling to unravel. By then, Bolivia—the Kurdish woman whose fingers had reached between his ribs and carved a path to his Andean heart—had vanished and left him with an intense thirst to understand the coincidences that tied them together. Perhaps she had gone back to Europe, or crossed the Bosphorus to return to Kurdistan—that imaginary patria her people were trying to rip out of history using bombs and flags. Sometimes he would read news about a Turkish air attack against the Kurdish population, cornered as it was in the dusty regions bordering Iraq. In those early dawns in winter, distance would make a silent film in his imagination: columns of fire and shattered earth rising out of the explosions and bombings, and he tried to remember her enjoying freedom, sheltered from the scythe of repression and death. Alone in his tiny apartment, Alfredo felt as if he were sinking under the long time that absence lasts.

Why did Boxeador kill himself? In those winter days of 1980, inexplicable things were happening throughout the entire Bolivian army—at the air force garrison in La Paz, at the navy units stationed in Tiquina, at the Tarapacá armoured regiment, at the northern Amazon regiments specialized in jungle operations, the Cochabamba airborne forces, the Chichas IV infantry regiment in the south. Perhaps there was no explanation, or perhaps the explanation was too obvious, too faithful to the country's historical pattern, too brutal to be accepted without the weapon of silence. Sixteen years later, in the middle of the snow, Alfredo was attempting to unravel the secret that had forced Boxeador to set the fire selector switch of his Belgian 20-round light machinegun not to the safety position, not to single-fire, but to the last one: burst mode. After settling more comfortably on the beaten earth floor of guard post number sixteen at the El Alto Air Base, Boxeador had blown out part of his head by firing a round of ammunition under his chin. As he wrote down these lines, Alfredo pondered for the first time that perhaps Boxeador hadn't committed suicide, that perhaps someone had killed him. Like Mamani, an Aymara soldier whose death no one protested, not in 1980, not ever. When his parents heard the news standing outside the garrison, they lowered their eyes, muttered their misfortune in Aymara, accepting the death with a deep fatalism, and walked away, taking with them their discreet tears, their quiet pain in the face of something they didn't understand in its full horror, trying to imagine the shape, the face, the mask worn by a State, a country that took the flesh of its flesh and destroyed and disappeared it. Alfredo recalled how each of their son's fingers had been tied with a rope and pulled out beyond the limits of pain, how he'd been interrogated through his agony about the whereabouts of some missing rifles. Gradually and methodically, they broke Private Mamani's bones one by one over the first days of his long death. Everyone, from battalion commander Major Trifón Echalar Miranda to Non-Commissioned

Officer Juan Barrón Huet, was responsible for that death. Despite the crime, all of them will go on with their lives as if nothing happened. No one will say anything. No one will demand an investigation, a judge, a verdict. No one, ever, because Private Mamani was just a poor *indio*, a *lari*, a sad Native who never existed because in Bolivia the law doesn't allow anyone to be born, grow up, get justice or die officially in Aymara.

Best not to think, Alfredo, best not to think. Sometimes ideas turn into curare and paralyse time itself. Some ideas make you seize, just like your arm, leg or heart may spasm when you try to swim across Lake Titicaca. Remembrance can weigh you down and pull you under, a swimmer struggling to stay afloat in the dense waters of history. Empty yourself, pack your mouth with ice, muffle your memory with rags, stop staring at your fingers and chewing on your hands—the same hands that on an August afternoon aimed a loaded rifle at a *chola* as she crossed a cobblestone street carrying her *huahua* on her back. Her steps were deliberate, containing the electricity, concealing the panic that urged her to seek cover, aware that if she took off running the soldiers would shoot her down. They were raiding a church where a terrified priest, wrapped in a sheep's wool sweater, still had the courage to defy the blind, infinite arrogance of the Bolivian State incarnated in the figure of Major Fatso Trifón Echalar Miranda. The *cholita paceña* was crossing the street in the midst of Narcogeneral Luis García Mesa's coup—her black felt hat tilted according to the occasion, her firm calves used to long walks through the Andes, her long *polleras* suspended from her waist tolling like serene woollen bells, and an *aguayo* wrapped around her back holding the light weight of a *bolivianito* who hadn't the slightest idea about that place where fate decided he'd be born, or about the collective history that would some day give him a face, a memory and an identity. It was shortly after noon, and the sun was bright in the clear, cold air of the Andean heights. In the distance, the polluting smoke-stack of the Viacha cement factory. For an instant, the priest of the Aymara parish could sense the major's sudden dis-comfort upon seeing his disproportionate forces: almost fifty well-fed soldiers each carrying two hundred cartridges of ammunition, ten thousand bullets at the command of a major of the Bolivian Air Farce, against the puny priest, who despite his noticeable pallor and outraged Spaniard demeanour held his gaze like a mongoose facing a snake. That morning around 11:00, two sections of the second company and half a dozen officers, including the battalion commander, had left the Air Base headed towards the church. The armed storm travelled in two blue buses and parked a few blocks away from the church. As soon as sol-diers began to pile out and split into two nervous columns along the sides of the street, locals began to seek cover behind every corner. Doors started banging, dogs were kicked into houses against their will, mothers screamed and shoved their children inside, businesses shut their doors, people hid behind windows, men were rushing, more doors banging, angry eyes, laboured breathing, cold sweat drip-ping down backs. History in those moments is heavy and vicious in the stomach; the nation, a desert in the throat. Soldiers covered all four corners around the church, another group of soldiers took position by the wood-and-brick gate, under orders to aim their barrels at everything that moved, to open fire—one shot after another—as soon as the order came. Realizing right then that she couldn't flee at the speed of a *warmi walaycha*, the *chola* took her caution across the street as if she were walking a tightrope across a swamp, hoping the alligators don't wake up. More than a dozen gun barrels were pointed at her, following her every step. The major knocked on the door. "Open up! Open up! We know you're in there!" And here the Scribe wavers, unsure of whether to write down in the name of history the foaming rage that had just been expressed. Did the major say, "Open up, turds!" or did he use a more forceful "fucking turds" or even a crass and cruel "Open the door, you son-of-a-whore priests!" Here your dedicated Scribe only knows for certain that the major never uttered a polite, "Please open, respected citizen, in the name of the law." The door didn't open right away. The major started knocking on the door with his folding-stock Belgian rifle with increasing force and fury, as if he just wanted to be done capturing all the seditious elements that attempted against the high interests of the nation. The personnel behind the bossy brute swiftly stepped aside to avoid a potential stray bullet from the rifle he kept pounding on the door of the house of God a few days after the coup d'état of July 17, 1980. After long, tense minutes, steps approached and the church door opened. The silhouette of a young woman appeared, perhaps a terrified novitiate who didn't dare make eye contact with the moustached leader of the uniformed pack. The major cinched his paunch and threw himself against the door, making the girl stumble backwards, and forced his way towards the altar. Alfredo and a dozen other soldiers entered behind the nervous officers, who began to inspect all the rooms one after the other, opening all doors starting with the sacristy in the front until they reached the priest's quarters in the back of the building. The priest followed them around not saying a word. They reached a room where, both delighted and dismayed, the officers discovered a manual Gestetner mimeograph next to a pile of freshly printed pages still smelling of wet ink. "Aha!" exclaimed the major, pouncing on his finding. "Why the hell do you keep doing these things? You dumb priest. Don't you know this is illegal? Why do you come to Bolivia if you're not going to obey the law?" He was yelling the way an unconvinced actor repeats his lines to impress the officers and soldiers under his command, convince them of his loyalty to the new regime. That's what he was getting paid to do—it was a shitty job but it guaranteed a good salary, housing, education for his children, and status in a country that had more in common with the misery of Haiti, Somalia and a hundred other countries, than with the advanced anti-communist Western democracies in whose name and cause the coup d'état had been carried out, a saving military action that instated a national reconstruction government as malicious and fascistic as only Bolivian dictatorships could be, with or without the military, with or without the mask of democracy. Alfredo had a glimpse of the flyers that had been left behind on the table, like birds with clipped wings. The major kept bombarding the priest with his rancid morning breath, his frenzied eyes bulging out of their sockets, blaming him more for making him lose sleep than for printing flyers about the resistance to the coup in the mining towns of Catavi, Llallagua and Siglo XX. The flyers included details about the intensifying air bombings against mining centres, soldiers refusing to shoot down the population—and being shot in the back by a superior—and manufacture and farm unions being reconstituted and already beginning their underground work in La Paz. The small notes, with all their insignificance and spelling tragedies, urged the population to resist. Now the puny priest—a slogan made flesh—resisted with equal measures of pluck and pallor the imprecations, profanities, threats and other verbal salvos coming at him from thick Major Trifón Chantón. During one of the major's pauses, the priest filled his lungs with as much oxygen as his church could fit, his face turned a colour that resembled communism but was in fact the colour of indignation, and unloaded a loud, "You have no right, no right at all to terrorize, to abuse, to kill people..." The major's eyes widened in surprise at the audacity of faith, enraged by such an affront. Private Cutipa could see a tiny blood vessel burst in the major's dilated eyes. The *chola* had succeeded in crossing the street a good while ago. While the major was mauling and pistol-whipping the daring, subversive mimeographer into a pulp, a neighbourhood dog—a *thampulli*, one of those bold, friendly, loyal and cheeky *ch'apicitos*, caring little about the transcendence and gravity of that moment in Bolivian history—walked up to a corner and lifted an unconcerned leg to mark its territory with a liquid signature. Before the mutt had finished satisfying its anarchic, renal impulse, its body seemed to jump up, hang in the air for a moment, then burst into a giant red splatter against the wall. At the roar of the gunshot the entire contingent of soldiers flattened against the ground, including the major, who thought his discovery of the subversive press had unleashed the communist savages' revenge, and they were now shooting from all sides. But there was only a single shot. Some of the soldiers stood up, scanning around for the origin of the shot. The street was still. Silence burned in their ears after the shot stopped ringing. A single soldier had remained standing on the steps to the church throughout the entire incident, his rifle hanging from his arm like a freshly lopped off branch. It was Private Calditos, standing stiff, bolted to the ground, watching the puppy refuse to die, how it gnawed at itself in pain and licked its blood in vain, its intestines scattered on the side-walk, trying to run away dragging his body by its front legs. The soldier looked down at his gun, not fully cognizant of the magnitude of his shot, and one of the officers pounced on him, his fists tight, his face contorted by rage.

"He called on one of his assistants with the voice of a troop commander and ordered, 'Bring me some *ají de fideos a la marinera!*' His carnal dagger once again demanded engage-ment in a new carnal campaign." A few years had passed since Alfredo had jotted down these lines, unable to decide whether to write the rest of the scene. What had begun as a letter to Susana San Miguel—who would surely be disap-pointed upon reading these meagre results—had become a sort of chronicle of Montreal winters. Outside, the cold travelling on the wings of the polar winds was sinking the city in a fifty-below silence. The shame he felt at needing to describe what those words meant—the banzeroid demand for a bowl of *fideos a la marinera*—made Alfredo skirt around being more explicit. "It's just a metaphor," he said to him-self, "a metaphor that will just upset the readers, perhaps even set them against the narrator, risk a premature aban-donment of these lines."

"Why don't you just describe what happens after," he asked me, his humble, anonymous and earnest Scribe, tasked only with transcribing the one thousand and one words Alfredo plots, scribbles, improvises, recalls and makes up. "Why me? You're the author of this."

"I'm not the author either," Alfredo replied. "All I do is dig in my memory and recover or bury details, sometimes with pick and axe, others with a toothpick. The real author of all of this is that pair of eyes you can see from this plain, those eyes staring right at us right now like two faithful suns, keeping track of every single line." (Hi Ponciano, hi Cardán, hi Mediopolvo! So now we've annoyed the officers of the Bolivian Air Farce, eh? This is just a story, you big *cerotes* wrapped in flags and uniforms! Only a *tacalo* would get upset che!)

"If you deny being the author," I protested, "why do you put your messages in parentheses like you just did? You've just distorted things by trying to smuggle in your little personal notes. People are going to think these stories are true and the characters we just described are real flesh-and-blood people."

"Look, Scribe, just start writing down that thing about Banzer and the bit with the *fideos a la marinera* and the dagger, because otherwise we're both out of a job. If I stop telling stories for you to write down, you'll have to look for another job. You're the one who's going to lose the most here, and whoever is reading us, if that's what you're worried about."

"Susana San Miguel, Marcelle Meyer, Amelia. All of them names whose light and voice brightened happier days." Alfredo thought about how much he needed metaphors, no matter how cruel they may seem. After two months of forced silence and narrative paralysis, he managed to convince the Scribe and inspire him to continue his work. (Despite his university degrees, the Scribe couldn't find a job that was more interesting than this tangled story.)

"That's not true! Please forgive us, dear readers. Alfredo is just lying here when he says I couldn't find other work options outside these writings. That's it."

Meanwhile, Susana San Miguel's letters were arriving in the island of Montreal like the distant noise of a fragile light plane manned by Fabián bringing correspondence from the South. The aircraft would slowly come into view, then start circling the lonely igloo. Alfredo would come out waving his arms like an excited ant welcoming the biannual visit from the plane, which would airdrop a large box filled with the victuals he'd need to survive in that island—the eye of the North Pole itself, the way he saw it. Then the propeller plane would take off and disappear again into the heavy curtains of low, cold clouds. Knowing the plane could stop coming any day, Alfredo was delighted to open the box, forgetting to put on his gloves in the blistering cold. He'd devour each word written by Susana San Miguel, while February spun around him in an ice-and-snow choreography, as if time itself was dancing in the cold and reconstructing every meticulous musical sentence from Prokofiev's intense *Montagues and Capulets*. Falling snowflakes seemed to arrange themselves following the movement of the bows on the strings, pushed by the powerful currents that emerged from the deep bowels of the trumpets. They would rise and fall in the air like small flocks of white birds, slowly forming the packed, uniform surface that brought Susana San Miguel's tight handwriting for hungry Alfredo to decipher, filling the uninhabited infinite space around him with echoes, trees, murmurs and voices.

Let's imagine again the unfinished metaphor in which our character's name is now María.

"Why weave a story about something that happened fifteen years ago? Soon it'll be twenty, fifty years. Why not use the strategy of pragmatism? Why not outline the central structure of a novel, what has been called for so long the Great Bolivian Novel? An inane, presumptuous dream, as if one could speak about the 'Great Bolivian Physics' or the 'Great La Paz Mathematics.' Let's assume for a moment that this is called 'The Great Bolivian Novel' even though none of what has been written may be great, or novelistic, or even Bolivian..." Alfredo reread the lines he had just penned in his notebook—where days and words gathered with no order or harmony, or rather, reflected the bustle of an existence filled with multiple referents, doubts and loyalties. Although he had the entire narrative structure on the tips of his fingers, he couldn't make up his mind about explaining everything that self-censorship prevented him from writing down. He would spend his time writing other things down, while his eyes registered the growing numbers of beggars in the Montreal metro, and both small and large groups of workers, students and unemployed protesting in the cold and snow. He was gradually beginning to recognize certain causes, until then unknown to him, seemingly unnecessary collective notions, such as those of patria, nation, or independence. Along with that, the conflictive shadow of national flags—he was beginning to see in the people around him the historical desire to be a nation, with the resulting foundation of a new country: Quebec. Winter days ran after each other like hockey players fighting over the puck that held Alfredo's memory and consciousness. One day, as he continued his committed, secret search for Bolivia, he stumbled upon a restaurant near the Beaubien metro where they made and sold *salteñas*—*salteñas*, near the North Pole! There is no word more magical and beautiful for a Bolivian abroad than the word *salteña*. A faraway voice burst in from the depths of his memory: a story from Grandfather Alejandro after a meal, hidden in a long-gone childhood. At the end of World War II—during the liberation of Paris and while Hitler was yelling into the phone asking if the city had burned—as they advanced on one side of the Arc de Triomphe, Allied troops noticed in the distance a long cane, a tall, thin mast hung outside a door on a side street. Someone had tied a minuscule white flag at the end of it. Chewing on a ball of gum, one of the soldiers read it as a sign of unconditional surrender, but once they arrived, they would learn from a Frenchman familiar with the Llajta that it actually meant *chicha buena* in good Cochabamban. Sitting in that Montreal restaurant on Rue Beaubien with two sovereign *salteñas* loaded with condiments, Alfredo was shocked and satisfied to hear news on the radio about the imminent extradition of the general, the ex-general, the gonorrhal Luis García Mesa—or was it Meza?—who would be transferred from Brazil to the frigid walls of the Chonchocoro jail. He choked on his *salteña*, on the news, on history. He thought about the ex-dictator's good fortune, who had sworn to stay in power until the year 2000, even if it cost the country a diet of *mote* and *chuño* heavily seasoned with bullets and repression. A photo taken a few days after the coup of July 17, 1980, showed the proud *generelelos* next to Johnny Walker's smiling face, one of his cabinet's most dedicated advisors. In the end, his megalodipsomaniac dreams had been reduced to a puppet regime, a nightmare that lasted under a year. It was lucky that gonorrhal García Meza was even still alive after all. He couldn't breathe. What would have become of that poor rearguard militiaman if he'd suddenly found himself—with all his devotion to Bolivian neo-Nazi groups—walking on some street in Berlin in July of 1940, if he'd been detained by two hefty members of the Nazi party eyeing his skin colour and Andean physiognomy with growing eugenic interest? But no, future president of the national reconstruction government and commander-in-chief of the armed forces Luis García Mesza—in whose ranks Private Alfredo Cutipa had courageously served with thousands and thousands of other conscripts—had been born in Bolivia, a country whose extraordinary historic and climatic conditions had enabled the mass production of military and civil despots whose temples history has bestowed with a wreath of coca leaves. Only in a fictional country could four mestizos intoxicated by *Mein Kampf*—poorly translated and more appallingly digested—start organizing Nazi groups under the ridiculous moniker of "The Grooms of Death."[11] What Alfredo didn't know was that, years later, the public stage would welcome a new group of Bolivians possessed by another kind of fundamentalism. They would arrive speaking English, inebriated by the most esoteric free-trade theories, bringing an entire neoliberal *k'hoñichi*, the same one that two hundred years earlier had justified the imposition of trade, coastal bombings, and piracy on the high seas in the name of freedom of navigation. The forward neoliberal graduates would never learn that despite free-trade, pseudomodernizing theological cosmetics, their country would continue to be the same old colony of Natives and mestizos oppressed, exiled, exploited and executed inside their own borders by a class of people who rinsed their mouths with the word "Bolivia."

"I start over. I find a name for you: María. And then I invent an encounter, always the first, always the same one, where my eyes converse with your fingers and your voice touches me and your laughter undresses me in what you call an exercise in desire and I name the desire of invention." The woman reread the note the soldier had given her without

---

11   A new incursion of history, entered by another scribe, notes that members of the Spanish Legion also consider themselves the grooms of death: "Viva la muerte y vivan las cadenas" ["Hail death, hail chains"], the specimens chant. To this we could add the sacred vows chanted by Canadian neo-Nazis before they attack immigrants.

looking at her or saying a word as she made her way out of the military base. She had just offered her visiting services to General Muñoz. She'd heard someone knocking at the door while his military saurian body snored buried under the sheets, bloated with alcohol and filling the room with a sour fog. She considered for a moment whether to open or not. She decided she was too tired and didn't want to see anyone. As if they had read her thoughts exactly, someone slid an envelope under the door. María read the instructions: she was to show up to work on a certain day at a certain time at so-and-so's house on such-and-such street. The note came with a cheque for $1,000 US signed by a vice-minister. She sighed and glared at the piece of paper bearing the emblem of the Ministry of Finance. Then, doing her best not to wake up the slumped air force general, she got up and ran naked to the bathroom, took a quick shower, got dressed, and left the narrow fermenting room at the El Alto garrison. On her way out, a young man in soldier's clothing handed her a note and, before she could register his features in her memory, he disappeared among hundreds of other soldiers responding to the bugle call for the morning's first formation.

The old colononel saw her enter the room. He paid little attention to the few vague pleasantries they exchanged, his gaze focused on the woman's hips as she undressed with no further preamble. The colononel dug in his pocket for his decrepit carnal dagger, which began to awaken at that commotion. He was sitting at an enormous desk covered with a white cotton cloth embroidered with birds and the inscription "From the wives' club of the Círculo Militar on the first anniversary of the national renovation. August, 1972." On the middle of the table was a candelabrum with unlit wicks, a bottle of white wine and a tureen full of freshly prepared steaming *ají de fideo*. On the improvised dinner table were two rock crystal glasses, two flat plates each with a set of silverware, cotton serviettes, a pitcher of water and two glasses waiting for wine.

"I won't be eating anything," said the woman. The old colononel, who had been dreaming of his presidential chair since 1977, was clad in his immaculate parade uniform loaded with all the insignia appropriate to an army general, including the secret addition of two additional stars that made him the de facto general of the general of generals.[12] He said nothing. Only a veil of dissatisfaction flashed in his eyes when he realized he didn't even have power of command over his drowsy sexual slug or over the woman, who was standing at the other end of the room and stared at him with the eyes of her breasts, naked and defiant. Former president Hugo Cancer felt all the physical emptiness of no longer having the power in his hands, no longer being called "commander-in-chief of the Bolivian army" or *"excelentísimo señor presidente de la república"* or "general blah, blah, blah." He couldn't help cursing his godson Juan Pereda for screwing everything up. In his remote years as president he'd never needed to pay for a woman. He'd had dozens of them, the most terrified, resigned little women overwhelmed by trends and provincial worries about what-will-people-say, some seeking the security of having a roof over their heads and food on their plates; others, charmed by the ceremonial graduation dagger from Colegio Militar Germán Busch, and later, the flaming promotion stars that gradually crept over his shoulders and his cap like shining golden *akatankas*. Now the aging dictator had to pay for

12   One of the scribes, after exquisite sherry-fuelled disquisitions, has suggested that instead of "general," this should read "general degeneral degenerate." The reader has the final say.

the disquieting fancies by which he tried to cling to the vestiges of his once-unquestionable power. Fortunately, he still had friends he had placed—in better days—in succulent positions within public institutions, people who owed him favours, active coreligionists in a few ministries. In public they supported his party, Acción Nacionalista, still financed by the United States; in private, it was a nostalgic fauna of old dictatorial glories. What this country needs is a strong hand. Such sombre characters now enabled him to pay for delicate little luxuries such as the woman who was visiting him. All without leaving the slightest compromising trace. "Fuck the newshawks! They'll get nothing from me!" It's not that easy for a seventy-year-old to convince a strong, young woman to do a naked "Ritual Fire Dance" and then contort her body into a fakiresque position on an armchair so as to make the most intimate part of her anatomy into a human plate in which to serve *fideos* that—seasoned only by the emanations and vapours typical of a landlocked country's submarine zones—would transform in a matter of seconds into a glorious *ají de fideos a la marinera*. The ancient colononel walked to one side of the room and turned on a sound system. Manuel de Falla rose up in the air in a black frock coat, sucking on a *mate de yerba*, sheet music under his arm, and gaucho bombachas—the finishing touch. He looked at the woman and raised an amazed eyebrow, then at the ex-dictator sheathed in his star-studded martial whites. The composer frowned in deep repulsion. "What the hell? This is disgusting," and immediately turned around and disappeared back into the music from which he'd come. The woman abandoned her body to the performance, went to sit at the table and watched herself from a distance executing a slow dance to the beat of the music before the colononel's clammy eyes. She settled down on the armchair as the ex-dictator tucked his serviette under his collar. Afterwards, she took a shower, lit a cigarette and left.

"No, this is not a text about dictators. It doesn't have to be a text about the dictator. This is the last territory I have left in which to reconstruct my affection. Outstanding lines and chapters have already been written in *No One Writes to the Colonel*, in *I, the Supreme*, in so many other books. I await the death of dictators with patience because I know on the other bank of the river there are hands and arms and eyes and voices waiting for them that have not forgotten how their final enjoyment of life, their breath was taken away. I also know that inside these lines I could make them die a slow, painful death. Tie them to a tree trunk teeming with carnivorous ants in the style of *La danza inmóvil* or *The Vortex*. Shut them up in the Ministry of the Interior cells, on Avenida Arce, make them fast on bread and water guarded by brutes and policemen reeking of booze who never change their socks. Turn them into hunger artists, starve them to emaciation on the bloody mattresses of the Panóptico de San Pedro. Force them to survive on minimum wage and let them sink every month into the dark mineshafts of anxiety. Exile them to Ulan Bator where they will be consumed by nostalgia. Subject them to the fugitive law. Stuff three copies of *Awake!* and *Watchtower* magazines in their pockets and drop them from a helicopter into a pack of hungry polar bears. Lose them in Rio's favelas wearing new shoes and pockets full of dollars. Make them walk a few blocks in the Bronx, Washington Heights or Spanish Harlem shortly before midnight, gold rings shining on their fingers and a kilo of coke tucked under their shirt. All of this is possible. An act of revenge? No. Sometime the staging of exquisite acts of atonement and death are possible in the midst of day-to-day things: Years after shooting down president Isidoro Belzu and displaying his executed body on the Palacio Quemado balcony, ex-General Melgarejo is killed in the dark by two bullets to the back while pounding on a door that remains shut in a small Peruvian town. After ordering the slaughter of dozens of miners and the execution of Ernesto Guevara, ex-general Barrientos climbs into his helicopter boasting of his victory, unaware that the Tío's fangs will open during his ascent and turn men and machines into a ball of fire, exacting the precise retribution his divinity deserves over the calm red tile roofs of the town of Arque. Following the successful coup d'état of 1980, after congratulating the soldiers at the El Alto Air Base—the launching point for airplanes loaded with bombs and bullets headed to mining centres—in the middle of the night ex-colononel Muñoz feels his heart stop as the Tío's voice starts to choke him, calling him down to the bottom of the final mineshaft. In the rigour of his dictatorship, mighty ex-general Banzer is a powerless witness to his son's death, as tragic as that of many assassinated under his orders. In the parsimony of power, ex-general Luis Arce Gómez had sentenced that, 'from now on all leftists should walk around with their will and testament under their arm,' unaware that years later he, too, would fall into gradual decomposition and misery, locked up in a foreign prison, searching in vain for a leftist he could curse for the inexorable weight of oblivion on his rib-cage. Persecuted and living on the run years after the overthrow of his government—a regime running high on cafeteria Nazism—ex-General Luis García Mesza is returned to his own country's prisons, where he watches the days go by in his cell until, one night, he notices a nauseating smell hanging over him, the rotting odour that can only come from decaying flesh. He realizes his cellmate is no ordinary delinquent but a soldier in a ragged blue wool uniform, his face torn up and rotten, dried up shreds of blackened scalp hanging over a single eye socket that stares at him under a military salute, his fingers pointing at the spot where his temple should be but is instead an empty space, a hole in his shattered skull. *'Buenas noches, mi general!'* The hollow sound of the subterranean salute causes blood to burst in the ex-general's body: his veins revolt, systoles mix up with diastoles, his pulse begins to fire in all directions, his lung cavities fill with fluid, and his orbits try to hold back the bursting eyeballs as blood starts flowing from his tear ducts. Ex-General Luis García Mesza, crumpled on the floor in a highland prison, bile oozing from his mouth, begins to die a brutal natural death on this page. Boxeador props him up and together they stumble away, walking slowly through the walls and iron fences of the Chonchocoro prison, one hundred fifty kilometres from La Paz, until they fade into the infinite darkness."

Only his shoes travelled across the night, rivers, seas, tragedies and deaths to look out onto the new landscape from the door of the plane. They imagined before them a vast desolate terrain at the other end of the world. He didn't know then—nor does he know now—that with his first step off the airplane that arrived in Dorval, Alfredo ratified all his previous deaths, the voyage across ethereal Styx that lies between La Paz and Montreal. During the aircraft's descent, as his feet felt the hydraulic whirr of the wheels preparing for landing, he saw through the porthole the contours of the land below, vast plains crisscrossed by wide fluvial branches, the wailing waters of all the displaced people in the world running down the Saint Lawrence, a dense carpet of naked tree branches, conifer forests and, every so often, sparse desolate houses anchored in the midst of the grey autumn. At most, there were bears, some Iroquois, and Constable Chrétien, a Royal Canadian Mounted Police officer who was killing time reading a short story called "The Queen's Hat." A stunning giant red pepper on his head, neatly pressed uniform and tall brown boots, holding stamps and forms in hand waiting for the aircraft to finish crossing the fantastic distance and land, exhausted, in that dusty place called Montreal. The eyelets of the travelling shoes blinked for a few moments, waiting to take in the landscape as soon as the door opened. Instead, they found the long boarding chute attached to the plane with Sheriff Chrétien's inquisitive eyes at the other end. By then he'd finished reading Kinsella's mimesis and, not finding it amusing at all, was imagining all the various ways in which he could tear the hair out of whoever had written such a detestable story.

"He would thus demonstrate that violence was the primary reason for Bolivia's existence." He'd been writing with that goal in mind at the rate of one word per day. He would write entire paragraphs, then erase them, like a Penelope waiting for his Ulisas to bring him the inspiration he needed to finish his crude scaffolding of words. But Ulisas was taking a while to arrive. (The name Ulisas sounds like a disease: "so-and-so got ulisas, they're like buboes on your lymph nodes..." so let's write down Elisa instead. By the way, it is very unlikely for a man to be named Penelope, so let's call him Pepe. Voilà: Pepe is waiting for Elisa who is supposedly coming back from a ten-year trip. Happier than a sperm cell in a broken condom, Pepe finishes his chapbook, neglecting to find a good ending.)

Alfredo realized that what he was actually trying to do was conjure up the obstacles history had placed in his path.

The same history that had dropped him in the middle of a labyrinth of the events, verbs and circumstances that prevented him from reconstructing himself, separating him further from Amelia in the other world and from Marcelle Meyer in this one. The only light he had left was Susana San Miguel's. It was as if he'd been the one who'd lost part of his head, not Boxeador. Alfredo searched in vain for the pupil, the word, the image he was missing along with the rest of a memory that was playing hide-and-seek through these lines. Or was it the opposite, that he was now filled to the brim with other identities and inner symbols? Over the weeks it took him to reach this line, Alfredo had managed to give shape to the main features of a character, María, a woman who within a few paragraphs had felt used and uncomfortable in the role she was supposed to play. She shockingly decided to abandon this story and these pages, while he sweated India ink trying to give more prominence and presence to the female character. Perhaps sensing her imminent departure, Alfredo spent an entire night trying to explain and convince María that the obscene former army officer who wanted to eat *ají de fideos* between her legs was important to the story because he served as a historical anchor point and mummification of the power and absolute bankruptcy and corruption in Bolivian democracy. María listened with growing impatience until she finally stood up. She brought her fingertips to her thumb to make a small cone or pyramid—gesture with which an easterner says to another, *"¡pero che... boludo!"*—and spat out:

"*Pinche* Alfredo, how does history ever serve me? History is always what stays in the past, it's just dust, it's nothing. Here the only thing that matters is what keeps moving forward. And we're the ones that keep moving. I want to keep moving forward, Alfredo, I don't want to die of nostalgia."

María had started raising her voice, almost at the edge of tears. "I can't look back! I can't accept the scene with the *fideos* with that rotten old man, even if he's an ex-dictator, no matter how important and metaphorical he is for you! What do you take me for, Alfredo? Just a plate you use and throw away? Is that what women are in Bolivian texts? *Los textos bolivianos*. And I say *bolivianos* and not *bolivianas*, because women have always been invisible to official history. Can't you see that the way you write makes you as *machote* as the ex-dictator? Don't you see? You're going to end up like the boy in that story whose head is cut off in the middle of the war between Moors and Christians, and when they finally manage to stick it back on, they realize they've put it on backwards. You're just like those coffee-shop socialists. As soon as they get home, they starting bossing their women around and send them to the kitchen with a slap in the face while the pricks just think and discuss about equality and justice. They can't see beyond the tip of their noses. Why do all the best intentions in this world end up going to shit?"

Alfredo said nothing while she spoke. She sat back down and smoothed her skirt down over her knees. What did she mean, he was being machete? And that thing about the boy with his head cut off? The last thing he felt like doing right then was to start doing bibliographical research and have to use footnotes on every page. A beheaded boy whose head is stuck to his trunk in a version of the Fierabras mess. Now they were both sitting on the edge of the bed in Alfredo's tiny room, saying nothing. It was snowing. He thought if he'd had a couple of candles to brighten the space as darkness fell, he could have perhaps recovered the magic he'd felt when he'd first imagined her. I start over. I find a name for you: María. And then I invent an encounter, always the first, always the same one, where my eyes talk to your fingers and your voice touches me and your laughter undresses me. He put his hand on her shoulder. She accepted it, a gesture of both acceptance and faith that things could be different even though they were both condemned to sail in the same ship. He brought her closer and embraced her, as resigned and hopeful as she was, searching for a solution inside his sigh. We turn serious, take some distance, know ourselves to be secret accomplices in what you call an exercise in desire and I name the desire of invention. How many times had he imagined her before using adjectives to delineate each one of her features, describe the sensuality of forms capable of all the verbs? María, María, our voices touch, caress, recognize each other across the night and the distance, play and chase and own each other and make promises. My voice sleeps with you, your hair shows me the way into the night that sleeps upon your breasts, I drink the primeval waters of yourpubwhydothingsneedtoendthiswaywhileitr ytoseduceyouusingwordsborrowedfromoldtextslikethatpas sageinLopedeVegathatreads "Wishing to be inside you, my lady, to learn whether I am loved..." The sudden phrase shocked and upset María. She recognized the words Alfredo was repeating like a parrot came from an old letter, and she jumped to her feet and told him to go to hell with no qualms or hesitation, told him to stick his letter wherever he wished because there was nothing in the world that could make her change her mind. She was officially abandoning this paltry novel. Alfredo begged, even offered to use her name as the title of his humble work, even if it meant plagiarizing a Colombian author in the process and inflicting deathly jealousy on the other María—María of the long dresses and even longer sighs. She'd stopped screaming despite his protests and complaints, but she kept shaking him and pelting his ears with even more fragrant, indigestible adjectives about the value of history and about how men were only good for looking back on and looking at from behind. Not necessarily good Christian words, but they worked. Alfredo stopped insisting, then suddenly leaned over and bit her on the thigh. Upon feeling Alfredo's moist teeth, her rage began to fade away. She started laughing under her breath while holding his author's head against her and moving it up closer, keeping it in contact with her skin, still laughing under her breath. Alfredo looked up for a moment and saw the flame of two candles appear out of nowhere. María's shoulders revealed themselves in the soft glow as she slowly unbuttoned her blouse, and Alfredo's lips set off in a long caravan of kisses through her body's sweet endless paths. Alfredo and María finally came out three days later—two sore tired bats emerging into the morning daylight. They had breakfast together at Café Le Damier at Bélanger and Saint-Denis and kissed each other goodbye on both cheeks, their faces saturated with the smell of coffee and fried eggs. A few hours later, she took her treasure chests full of words and set off with a theatre company that had offered her a more significant and dignified role than to serve as sexual object for a decrepit army scoundrel, all because of a tightly wound Scribe. A week later, she began rehearsals for a role in *Amerika*, a play based on the work of a Czech writer who falls in love with his translator, Milena Jezenska. Outside, the snow turned Montreal into a vast white page in which all stories were possible.

The world is a continuum of tastes, scents and sounds. Scents, sounds and bones? Bones, fleas and humans?

Urrrrrf. It's tough. It's tough. We never sleep, or rest. We just exist. We can exist from two perspectives: on foot or on land. On two legs or four legs. On land, we observe and meditate, breathing in and moistening the earth with our snout. The rest of the time we run, smell, lick, bite, mate, watch, recognize, track, bite again, follow, chase, cohabitate, I mean live in canine sin and howl and want without really knowing why or for what. Not that we ever think about time all that much. Likely I wouldn't have even the slightest sense of time if it weren't for Cipión and Berganza, who started chatting one night and brought into our canine world all the time-related concerns that are unique to humans. The things that until then had no connection whatsoever to our everlasting golden age, where only children and succulent bones were kings and masters of our loyalty and affection. I wasn't resting last night. I just listened to those things that go down the street, roaring and growling with blazing eyes, making their short, swollen rubbery feet turn and turn. Sometimes the beasts will attack and leave one of us ripped open in the middle of the street. The humans climb in and out of them like it's nothing, but as soon as we get near them, grufff! the lights go out all of a sudden. Other comrades, I mean other canrades also let their voices be heard: they bark, howling in delight, greeting the night, asking humans to let them in or out, begging for a bone, asking for the freedom to go play, listening to the sounds of the moment. They celebrate at the top of their lungs when a door opens and the humans arrive after being announced by their own scent and the sound of their steps and their keys that sing secrets through the doors' eyes. We bounce and wag without rest, or try to scare away any human that threatens our family's den, risking the occasional stone that may punish our flanks. Canrades check their voices—high- or low-pitched bursts of air issue from their canine throats—and watch the night and its various regions of invisible light and clarity. This is the blind time when the air is filled with the round, thick aroma from some females' hindquarters, real rumps that call us with an indescribable force to practise the best exercise a mammal has ever been tasked with. Sometimes the flurry of activity leads to loud fights, clashing fangs, split ears, snouts dripping with angry foam and all sorts of brave gestures and elegant offences. The most important thing is not to surrender—even the hairiest fighters with the most impressive teeth sometimes wind up exhausted from running and fighting. There's Kaliman, always chained up, rarely allowed to leave the house, and when he does, he spends more time fighting than enjoying the fruits of his battles. Mmmmmmph! I've also enjoyed the blind, inexplicable pleasure that follows those skirmishes.

I wag my tail, bark, whimper, smile, beg. Scratch at the door. They open the door. I dash out. Stop, sniff, look. Feel. The vast earth that supports us is still. The street is quiet and I fill my lungs with a symphony of smells, wafting invitations, meals, humans, fluids, distances. I'm not hungry yet but I'm always ready. Something is crawling through the fur behind my ear, bites me with microscopic jaws. I sit back on my hind legs and lean my head sideways...aaaaah! It feels so good to scratch! ¡Gracias a la vida que me ha dado tanto! I yawn, stretch my front legs, curl my elegant tail. Shake. Greet the day with my voice. Other voices respond by barking in the distance. That's Bobiscu, the shepherd, true king of the small humans who haven't learned how to be mean or throw rocks at us yet. I suspect those humans mistake us for their siblings and think we're alike—there's no difference between dogs and humans their age. We're the same. I walk up to the wall, lift my leg and say in my liquid language, "I live here." Lest someone decide to encroach upon my human dogs and my territory. I listen to the day, my ears perked up, my nose shiny, my eyes alert.

There is an entire world of smells before me. I walk up to the church, always sniffing the air, marking my space, christening every corner and post with my name. Sometimes they leave excellent bones outside the church entrance. The time Cipión and Berganza spoke about is nothing more than this very instant. After I urinate I'm ready to own the place. But then, suddenly, fire, deep fire, a furious spear skewers straight through me. Oh, Berganza! Who will bark for me tonight? Could this burning feeling be pain and death? Aoouuuuuuuu! Aooouuuuuuu!

Scribe! Scribe! Where did you go? What the hell? Why do you throw a talking dog in the middle of a serious story? SCRIIIIIBE!!

He tried different ways to write, to talk the way a dog would. Perhaps unaware that he was doing so. He spent three Sunday afternoons sitting outside in a small park behind the Museum of Fine Arts on Sherbrooke Street, at the bottom of the Mountain. The property owner's last wish, perhaps in the late nineteenth century, was to donate it to the city of Montreal. He wanted to give dogs on the island a place to recover their ancient wolf-like freedom, burn up all the energy they'd accumulated penned up over long winter months inside the neighbourhood's apartment buildings. They would run, bounce, play, bark at the top of their lungs, chase each other around, sniff each other point-blank, wag tails, pose majestically jutting out their chest and tensing every single one of their canine, urban muscles. Sometimes there were courtships and sudden passions that bewildered their owners with their cheerful lack of modesty. A debauched Chihuahua would run around madly after a Great Dane. There were accidents and eager indulgence—a passionate dog confusing fore and aft while trying to hump a female. Some noses, not used to the furry social interaction, simply could not tell one gender from the other. Only puppies would do their own thing, diving and rolling around in the snow, looking for imaginary sticks. Some dogs wore scarves; some of the smaller short-haired ones had custom-knit wool vests. Alfredo suddenly realized that in all his years in Montreal he'd never seen a street dog, not even a lost dog. Nowhere on this island had a single dog made the qualitative leap from *chien-en-soi* to *chien-pour-soi*, the way dogs would roam in absolute freedom among the imaginary windmills of his childhood. He recalled that sometimes those dogs—spiritual children of the Paris Commune—would stand firm in front of him with egalitarian eyes. Did the dog shot to death outside the El Alto church enjoy that canine lucidity in its last moments?

On a Sunday afternoon, coming home to his third-floor apartment on rue Cartier, near Papineau, *notre cher Alfgedó, oui, Alfgedó*, saw a *fantóm par terre waiteeng for heem at dee fgont door, oui, oui*. When he saw the person curled up in the hallway, he thought it was a homeless person seeking temporary shelter from the winter. Or a drunkard sleeping it off on the floor, his head hidden under the high collar of a worn winter coat. He inhaled a couple of times, checking for alcohol odour in the air. Nothing. Only a light tobacco smell wafted up from the grey coat. He tiptoed up to the door, trying not to startle the body sleeping in foetal position. He reached the front door and grabbed his key. As he touched the metal tip to the door lock, he heard a weak, hesitant voice: *"Alfgedó?"* The body stirred and slowly came to. The person stood up leaning against the wall, revealing the tired face of a woman whose features slowly issued forth from the fog of his memory.

"Alfgedó... c'est toi Alfgedó?"

He thought he recognized her voice. What did she look like? "A woman with long black hair and eyes of grey coral." Yes, it was her! But her long hair was gone. Now it was short and pointing in all directions, as if each strand were raising its hand requesting the floor in a vanishing constitutional assembly. Was she the woman he'd met almost two years ago? He had decided to buy socks the colours of the Bolivian flag as a gesture of silent protest against the viceroy elected president of the colony named Bolivia. He remembered how he'd put them on—almost enraged, almost aggressively—his best garb for all the Latin American parted announced in posters in Côte-des-Neiges corners, at cafés on Saint-Denis, in bus stops.

Was it she? Was this the woman who'd spoken to him about the liberation of Kurdistan? Was she the woman who didn't have a patria but dreamed of having one, while he had one whose symbols he loathed with all his might? She looked at Alfredo expectantly, not completely recognizing him, or perhaps somewhat afraid of being recognized. After all they'd only spent a short amount of time together. Was this the wrong apartment? Was this the man who used to amuse her with his horrendous French and his tragicomical national explanations? The man who'd kept a straight face while saying he was a registered member of the glorious Broken Bloc? The man she'd held and loved an entire night, shortly before leaving Montreal, not minding, rather enjoying his inexperienced eager hands on her breasts, letting herself be carried by the Amazon River of kisses flowing from his mouth, delighted to be feeling life in her deepest self before setting off on yet another journey in the name of the cause, not knowing whether she'd come back to the island alive.

"*C'est toi, Alfgedó, Alfgedó?... Mon gauchiste-caviar?*"

"Is that you...Bolivia?"

He remembered the smell of gunpowder and smoke in her words. And this is just a rhetorical figure because Alfredo believed he remembered clearly the perfume she'd been wearing the night they met. (What was it?)

"Yes, it's me, Alfredo. Bolivia, is that you? *C'est toi, la femme du Kurdistan?*'

"*Sí, sí, c'est moi!*"

"The one who ran away with my favourite socks?"

He immediately regretted saying that. You cheap miser! To be thinking about your famous antipatriotic socks right now, when the woman you've spent months looking for all over the island is standing right here in front of you *¡Tacalo tenías que ser, che!*

"*Alfgedó! C'est toi...c'est toi!*"

"Come on in, come on in," Alfredo urged, inviting her inside. She stood up as if she were carrying centuries of exhaustion on her shoulders, then sat down to drink the hot chocolate he'd prepared to take away the February chill, always nipping at your toes. They said a few words but mostly observed each other, trying to recognize in one another's features any signs or evidence of what and how much they had changed, what still remained in their memory of what they each had been to the other during the short time they'd shared so long ago. He recognized Marseille in her accent. She laughed, reminiscing about the morning she left, stealing Alfredo's tricolour socks as a memento. And for the cause. He told her he'd looked for her month after month in every single Montreal neighbourhood, every corner, looked for her even in the old winding Quebec City streets, in Toronto's linguistic labyrinths, in the mazes of bars and ports in Halifax. He had waited for her at the tattooed, knife-scored tables of Winnipeg's only hamburger joint, looked for her in every train car of the

Edmonton-bound iron horse—the miniature train that traverses the rugged, dense geography of the Canadian Shield across the endless prairies flaming in the sunset—and called at doors in places where no one could ever give him even a sliver of information, only met him with mistrust. Alfredo didn't have much time to talk: after drinking her hot chocolate, she got up, walked over to the bed and collapsed into a deep sleep that would last three consecutive days.

Upon awaking, struggle against an extreme sensation—enormous weight upon eyelids. The first thing in sight was the bedroom ceiling and a blurry shape, perhaps a giant fly in the middle of the washed-out space, suspended and trapped in fate's invisible spider threads; then, trying to think back to what had led to such a painful and pitiful physical condition. Reaching out for the self next to that circumstance, cookies—Christie Premium Low In Fat—offered by the nightstand to the right of the narrow hospital bed. Past the cookies were spherical shapes identifiable as citrus fruits. An attempt to reach out farther and explore the limits of the immediate universe, thwarted by a pinching sensation in a nerve. Something piercing through under the skin, deep inside in veins that ran, not with blood, but with slow asphalt rivers amidst thick curtains of rising vapour, asphalt poured and raked and rolled slowly by pavers despite the frigid winter temperatures to cover potholes left behind by salt and ice, as Alfredo walked to the Jean-Talon Market, where immigrants from every tongue and every latitude perform their silent work: the gradual integration of local Canadians into the spontaneous cosmopolitanism newcomers have built one drop at a time in Montreal. Charm their palate, subjugate their senses, please their taste buds with subtle delights from cultures from faraway horizons—a seemingly steady and effective mechanism. The life of many Quebeckers had irreversibly changed after their first morsel of a whimsical cherimoya, the first sweet taste of prickly pears melting in their mouth—a constellation of seeds that opens into an intricate, sugary, cosmic explosion, arousing images of unfamiliar geographies, other eyes to see the world, imaginary memories of freckled-faced lovers. Many unions—some of the flesh, some of the spirit—had undergone slow ripening among Chinese lettuces, Vietnamese herbs, Punjab curry and delicate rice noodles from the Philippines. Women and men who had arrived on this island from faraway regions of the planet would devour each other in an urgent kitchen table feast, while they prepared an avocado salad with minced onions and tomatoes, drizzled with lime juice, olive oil, salt and pepper. In bedrooms all over the island, the blood of men and women bloomed on flushed faces and necks, on sweaty chests, next to the first eroticized yuccas with a few drops of lemon juice. Seeing a small fresh fig open ripe and dark and sex-like on their fingertips, many construction workers with unruly moustaches and callused hands would stop in the middle of the street, suddenly blushed, moved by the fruit's carnal revelation, by its sweetly opened flesh, their eyes flooded by gusts of memories issuing forth from the deepest corners of their love and remembrance. This is the way—Alfredo thought as he wandered through the market stalls looking for the best eggplants, to roast and serve to the woman who'd come to his door all the way from the war and bombs and the ghost of an imagined patria—this is the way we will succeed in founding collective identities that favour all gastronomic differences. *Vivent les papilles libres! Vive le Québec ivre!*

Gibberish. That's all his thoughts were while he watched the city workers filling a pothole with steaming asphalt and gravel, working at a good pace and questioning one another in loud peppery words about whether they'd slept with a woman the night before.

Bolivia stayed in the refuge of Alfredo's room for almost two days, collapsed in bed, overwhelmed by the ruthless gods of shrapnel and gunpowder causes, feeling that although her body was here, on the island of Montreal, her soul was still meandering through Istanbul's Spice Bazaar and Frankfurt's cold avenues. Meanwhile, Alfredo was itching to hear about everything that had happened during her long absence. He couldn't tell if he was simply curious or if he was just happy to see her again. Walking among the pyramids of fruit, mint and sweet potatoes at the Jean-Talon Market, he felt like dancing but not sure to what, an enlightened devil, a *kusillo* nimble on the snow, feeling that Bolivia's arrival had warmed even the air, taking the harsh chill out of the morning air. Thanks to Bolivia, his heart's winter and nostalgia were subsiding—the wind blowing through the streets chilled his gloveless hands and wrapped around his naked head, rubbed against his large ears. Thanks to Bolivia, winter felt less cannibalistic. "No… This can't be. A Kurdish woman named Bolivia…" he said in endless amazement as he realized that yes, such an encounter was indeed possible on this island, surrounded by the powerful arms of the Saint Lawrence River, with its large chunks of ice balancing on the current, the ice that was now nipping at his toes, feet so remote he was unable to make out their shape, unable to focus on the body's boundaries, unable to see later that day the spider of fate descend upon the trapped fly that swung from the pale ceiling. Looking towards one side of the room, the corner where the horizontal plane of the ceiling met the verticality of the wall—there was something there. A shape, a shadow, something that remained still, perhaps looking in this direction, or calculating the right moment to sink its furry arachnid fangs into the winged insect trapped in the centre of the room, or descend this way and find arms, face, bite into an eye, the only one allowing the light into the well where memories slept. Gradually scents began to reveal what was happening all around—it smelled of therapeutic dreams, heart attacks and surgically removed nostalgia cells. A weak voice kept repeating a series of *"ayoye...ayoye...ayoye... ayoye..."* like some sort of drunken, dancing crab. Alfredo keeps walking through the market, a dancer celebrating a feast day by the sacred lake. "Sweet Bolivia has returned." *"Faites attention à la marche, monsieur!"* He looked over to see whose voice was scolding him and found a creole woman staring in frustration as her broccoli rolled down across the ground. *"Oh, caramba, quel brute je suis! Madame, s'il vous plait excusez-moi!"* With his dancing enthusiasm, Alfredo's sudden turn among the people at Jean-Talon Market—a little waka-tokori step, a rhythmical move forward, then backwards to the sound of rockets and horns—had caused the vegetables and roots to spill behind him. The owner of the broccoli was a Haitian woman. After carefully picking up the fallen produce, Alfredo's musical register changed, this time he tried to dance caporales, a type of dance in fashion in a Bolivia that was rocked by whips and bullets *(in Bolivia? how was he going to establish the difference between that flatulent, ungraspable concept of nation and the woman sleeping in his bed at that very instant? Which one was more important? That is, which one was worthy of being named with the honour and elegance of an upper case letter? And which one should remained confined to the lower case? He thought of discussing the issue with the Scribe but decided the matter was his sole responsibility. So, at this very instant, Alfredo faces a wide, invisible audience of ten million Bolivians, and clad in lluchu and tie, mestizo, mixed, trilingual, under the spotlights he grabs the microphone and gives a solemn official*

*declaration: "ahem! ahem! cough… cough… onetwothreetesting-
testing: My fellow tacalo citizens, I hereby present the following official declaration, colon, next line (:) Whereas the undersigned has
been subject to circumstances beyond his control, he hereby declares
for all judicial purposes that his birth took place in an unspecified
geography completely unbeknownst to the undersigned; Whereas
the aforementioned fact has been evidenced by his first reaction,
namely, inconsolable wailing upon the exact moment of birth, subsequent to delivery from the womb, due to a brutal smack on the
bottom which forcefully extracted him from profound existential
and territorial cogitations; Whereas the consequences of being
birthed in a specific location cannot be attributed to the noble kingdom of the birds, represented herein by their attorney the stork;
Whereas the birth of the undersigned was in its stead the result of
physical ardours unleashed by the beneficial outpouring of* Punata
chicha, *the single and symbolic corn practice that enables the
unmasking and liberation of all Roman Catholic Apostolic self-con-
trol; Whereas the undersigned has suffered the emotional consequences of a severe case of acute homonymia which threatens to
confound his loyalties due to the double and multiple connotations
of the sound and name 'Bolivia'; Namely, (1) as a concept of origin,
birth and languages, there exists a geographic region known by the
name of Bolivia; (2) As of a recent unspecified date, said name contains within it a second, affective concept, due to the existence of a
physical female person on the island of Montreal also named
Bolivia. In view of the foregoing, and in consideration of the ethereal, windy, ungraspable and unstable qualities of the concepts of
national identity and geographical origin, and in consideration of
the human qualities, tenderness, companionship and emotional
presence of a woman named Bolivia, the undersigned subscribes
this duly notarized and registered document and hereby resolves…
RESOLVES…resolves! Article 1. Sole Paragraph. It is hereby
ordered by irreversible decree that the human being shall heretofore*

take precedence over the abovementioned ethereal concept. The conceptual apeiron of what is designated as the nation shall heretofore be secondary to the primary human manifestation of affection, and said physical person shall heretofore be named 'Bolivia.' The conceptual and invisible notion, the fancy of a viceroyalty, the colonial construction and functioning of the aforementioned republic shall heretofore be named 'volibia.' Signed in the City of Montreal, in this month of February in the year of our Lord 1995,) a type of dance in which one person pretends to be the foreman—the slave driver, whip in hand, forcing slaves to work, always perfecting his methods of inflicting pain. Alfredo tried to turn his ankles out, as though he were wearing ankle bells ready for feint steps and jumps. The Haitian woman stared at him while rearranging her broccoli in her basket, puzzled by what he may have been trying to convey through his pirouettes. Perhaps he was possessed by ancient gods. After reflecting for a moment about the minor accident, Alfredo stopped moving. He stopped playing a caporal because the practice suddenly struck him as impossible and awkward, stripped of its historical context. He turned into a run-of-the-mill guy, a *caserito* peacefully wandering through the market stalls, surrounded by vegetables, looking for eggplants of a lilac sheen, dark as the night that seeped through the window and made him shiver. The light was ill. As the fly and the spider were beginning to fade in the growing twilight, a nurse walked into the room and made the fly burst into an iridescent halo. Seconds later the spider of fate, curled up in the corner waiting for asleep to arrive, was suddenly lit up by the bright shapes of hockey players running around and armed with their sticks. *Hockey Night in Canada.* Another attempt to focus on things in the room—only shadows moving around were visible. The other eye, the blind one, was covered with a bandage; bones were still running through with murmurs, the echo of someone tapping on the counter at Fromagerie Hamel, a woman ordering a quarter pound of goat cheese. When it was his turn, he ordered some blue cheese, the most suitable for reading the old modernists and to eat with a fake *marraqueta* and *café con leche*. He wandered through the neighbourhood and found himself at the corner of Jean-Talon and Saint-Laurent. Possessed by an irresistible idea, he headed west to the Kurdish social centre for refugees. All tables were empty except for one: four men with fierce moustaches and nostalgia in their eyes were sipping steaming green tea out of plastic cups, watching on a small TV a video Alfredo thought he recognized as the one they'd been watching the first time he'd stopped in looking for Bolivia. On the screen, a group of women and men clad in beautiful costumes were performing a folk dance on a stage, surrounded by an excited audience, accompanied by powerful drums and a small flute similar to the one used by snake charmers. The music filled the place with its penetrating, undulating rhythm. He was shocked to see all the men were wearing the infamous tricolour socks. He also noticed tricolour socks for sale behind the counter, bags and bags of patriotic socks along with the usual banners, jerseys and coffee cups with the red, yellow and green of the Bolivian flag—or rather, the Kurdish flag. They were smoking and focused on the television when Alfredo jumped in front of them screaming, "Bolivia! Bolivia? You remember Bolivia? *¿Se acuerdan?* Do you? Yes? No?" They stared at him with a mix of interest and surprise, perplexed by what the effusive man was screaming at the top of his lungs. He pointed at the screen showing the close-up of a woman. "Bolivia! Bolivia! *J'ai trouvé Bolivia*, I found her, *Ich habe*, damn, how do you say in German, *les amis, écoutez! J'ai trouvé ma femme, ma Bolivie et merci à vous tous!*" They shook their heads, not understanding even a shred of what the gesticulating dancer was saying, trying to describe and swear in vain the depth of his joy upon having found the most beautiful damsel in the world again. He'd figured his attempt to share his sublime happiness had failed and then the door behind the counter opened and a Kurdish man Alfredo recognized walked in—or at least he thought he'd recognized him from the days he'd gone to the café almost daily to ask where Bolivia might be. The man also recognized him. He frowned and started screaming, gushing words that electrified the four men sitting at the table. They jumped to their feet, tensed up like springs. Alfredo was stunned. "¡Qué es lo que pasa! *Mais quoi?* What's happening here?" The man giving orders felt obliged to translate his frenzied words: "*L'espion c'est lui! C'est lui le salaud! De spiee, de spiee!*" Now the four men at the coffee shop were perplexed by their compatriot's screaming in French as he pointed at Alfredo, who turned around to check if the enraged man was pointing at someone else behind him. He was getting ready to explain that he was not a spy at all, him a spy for god's sake—stopping to notice the sound of the word and its vowel, the "e" in the word *espía*, "e" like extremely happy, which was applicable in his case. He was getting ready to share the reason for his happiness with the anxious group of bearded men who'd fixed their dilated pupils on him, but he didn't manage to utter a word because suddenly they jumped on him, picked him up and threw him against the wall like a tomato. The screaming man, who seemed to be in charge of those eight arms of Kali, leaped to the entrance and flipped the door sign to *Fermé*. From inside, the door now read *Ouvert* and Alfredo thought the surprise attack would now lead him to the gates to the afterlife. The owner turned the lights off and cracked his knuckles as Alfredo fell to the floor again like a flattened pizza. He was in Bolivia again, that is, in volibia, and Boxeador was pounding on him with his harsh welterweight fists, representing volibia in the Bolivarian Games organized by Great Gorilla Banzer. His fists kept multiplying and punishing his body. He yelled and screamed, trying to explain, but his attackers couldn't understand any of the languages he used to try to communicate with them. Alfredo slipped away for an instant as agile and panicked as a fish. He found a temporary shelter in a corner between shelves full of cups, socks and newspapers. He ripped some socks out of their bags and waving the colours of the sacrosanct national flag, he screamed in despair: "Stop, stop! Man, I'm volibian. Goddammit, I'm Bolivian!" This seemed to enrage them even more. Perhaps it was his swearing, or perhaps because he'd disgraced the colours of their imaginary Kurdish patria and was now bombarding them with bags of socks, emptying the shelves, hurling anything he could grab, trying to contain the mortal charge of the Kurdish cavalry. A chair came down crashing on his head and left him stumbling, bleeding and stunned. A smart bomb of a fist zeroed in on its radar and came down lightning-fast on its target, making Alfredo see the first summer fireworks on Jacques Cartier Bridge as his eyeball bounced and haemorrhaged inside its socket. As the impact made him fly through the air, he realized the Scribe was doing nothing to get him out of his eggplant pickle. He yelled at the Scribe while writing down the following lines: "Goddammit, do something! Do something! Can't you see they're beating me into a pulp?" And then they both arrived at a solution, a heresy, which is the mother of necessity, or necessity is the mother of eretics—the Scribe was neglecting grammar and spelling as he was writing this text, stunned and frightened by the uneven fight. He didn't remember the exact spelling, and he didn't have time to go back and write the missing "h" on the last heretic strikes that were about to issue from Alfredo's swollen lips—at the moment he needed all the help he could get from the grammar monkeys. The Scribe exerted his imagination, went back in time to the summit of Mount Hizan, gathered all the power in his lungs and jotted down an incantation that Alfredo immediately cried out: "*Sharafnâma peshmerga! Sharafnâma peshmerga!*" As soon as he did, the hailstorm of blows stopped pelting him, and he took advantage to wriggle away like an earthworm that knows its place. His assailants were stunned by his screams and looked at each other, then looked for an explanation all over the floor where Alfredo had just been rolling around like a corn kernel on a millstone. Alfredo thought about Bolivia—the woman, not volibia, his country of origin. He gathered what remained of his pitiful forces deep inside his battered being, somehow managed to stand up and, fooling his undeserving adversaries, stumbled out of the coffee shop. He flagged down a taxi who offered to take him to the hospital, but he gave his address and, because Allah is truly magnanimous with the infidels, he made it home alive, albeit as broken as a guitar that has been thrown from the eighth floor of the Jean-Talon Hospital, where he woke up alone and without the slightest idea of what may have happened to his eggplants. It was day now and in the light he could make out the blurry sunglasses and scarf covering the head of a woman who'd been sitting quietly by his side. "*Alfgedó? Mon amour*, are you better? can you 'ear me? *C'est moi, ta Bolivia.*"

"After the explosion it rained fingers, pieces of hands, legs, joints, shreds of skin, hair and metal, twisted and unrecognizable, all wrapped in dense phosphorous and nitrate smoke, and then you could still see tiny droplets of blood suspended in the dusty air. There were seventy-six dead and a hundred wounded after the explosion that shook the centre of Colemerik, a Turkish city located, as you say, at such a distance from this world that in your imagination there is only dust, sand, maybe a few camels, short columns of dust rising up in those corners of the world every time someone falls and dies muttering words in a language you don't understand. But no, Alfredo, over there is just like here. People worry about the same things: groceries, children, the weather, celebrations, family. People are born, get married, love, suffer, dream and die, just like here. No, maybe the difference is that where I was born, people live but they don't get the chance to be who they are. The law prohibits Kurds from being Kurdish; in Turkey using our language is illegal. They don't even let them die in peace because they kill them before their time comes. True, life conditions are different, but over there it's just like here. People live dreaming of having their own country. No, no, don't laugh. It's true, Alfredo. Things are just like here, people are people. Since that explosion in Colemerik nothing has been the same. Some of our movement's leaders were assassinated. Most of the comrades in charge of operations in Turkey and Iraq died in that dreadful bomb hidden in a car that I, I parked myself on a street in Colemerik following instructions from the military wing in our party. And then I realized they were following me. They'd been following me since I left Montreal. People in the movement were the ones spying on me. We've been infiltrated, Alfredo, we've been betrayed. They've betrayed us! Now we live in a permanent climate of terror. No one trusts anyone. There are terrible divisions. People carry guns even to go to the bathroom. There are new factions, and factions within factions. Our history, our language no longer guarantees solidarity, loyalty, security the way they used to. Entire sectors of the organization have disbanded in Germany, France, even here in Montreal. Fear and paranoia have come all the way here. And I'm scared, Alfredo, I am scared for you, because of what they did to you. And I'm scared for me. What's going to happen now?"

Alfredo saw tears shining down Bolivia's cheeks while she told him how Kurdish people were surviving storms of hatred and betrayal. They were persecuted and imprisoned in Germany, tortured, beheaded, castrated by Turkish security, bombed by the Iraqi government, by troops armed by the same empire. And yet, in spite of it all, in that promised land—the mythical Kurdistan, which did not exist except in the imagination of those who believed it did—people chatted over a cup of coffee, got married, laughed, had children. At first he thought she was crying over how dreadful he looked lying in a hospital bed, his head wrapped in bandages and his right eye buried under antibiotics, cotton pads and gauze. Beside his bed, a metal rack held the clear intravenous fluid feeding plastic tubes inserted in veins on the back of his hand. She may have been crying for him, for the state he was in due to the frenzied insecurity and terror of a few of her fellow Kurds. Or perhaps she was crying for her friends, the human fragments blown up through the air that afternoon in a city shaken by an explosion that would forever echo in her memory. Perhaps she was crying for him and his people, for everyone who had been baptized one way or another by the fire of their patria, persecuted by the harsh shadow of flags and causes demanding rivers, lakes and oceans of foam and blood.

During his convalescence, he noticed his ability to focus on the contour of objects was improving slowly. He didn't know what day it was or how long he had been in that condition or how Bolivia had managed to find him. She was there, telling him almost in a whisper what had happened during her years of absence in a voice that at times broke with sorrow, trying to contain unstoppable tears.

To tear days out of minutes, abolish the passing of these hours, chisel words out of silence. A violent exercise. Writing these words in his hospital bed, Alfredo realized he was starting on the same path again, the same falls and frustrations due to his incompetence with words. He was witnessing once again the constant exodus of the written word. He believed every verb or adjective he added to his writings moved him a millimetre closer to peace. He imagined the difficult route at the end of which he would find himself facing a stern, frowning guard at the door that separated identity from history, or history from identity, as seen from the other side of the bleak entrance. And even though he couldn't see what waited on the other side, he was certain there were people behind that door hoping to cross it in the opposite direction. From his bed, he looked towards the door again and saw Bolivia walk in, as she did every morning, bringing him the first apple in history, two smuggled croissants and a cup of *café con leche*. With no clear plans, Alfredo set off into yet another day of injections and words at the hospital.

During one of their long afternoon conversations at the hospital, Bolivia admitted with a faint embarrassed smile that she had indeed taken his patriotic socks the morning after their first night together, when she left his apartment and Montreal. "I had to say something. I was supposed to explain my activities, inform our local leaders if I'd made contacts that could help our cause. How could I explain to the comrades that I'd just left with you that night because I wanted to sleep with you? I couldn't tell them I liked you, that from the very moment I saw you walk into that church basement surrounded by fragrant food and loud music, I could already tell something was going to happen between us. I could have told them I'd spent the night dancing with you and later kissing you without caring about what was happening in our Kurdistan right then. But I don't think that was true. I think it was actually fear. I was just scared and I wanted to be with somebody, I wanted someone to love me, to make me feel I wasn't dead yet, that I was still part of this world, because I already had my plane ticket to go back to the war that following Monday. I was going to Paris first, and then to Turkey. We had a lot to do in Ankara and I didn't know if I'd ever come back to this city, if I'd still be breathing a year later, if I'd still be able to see my toes touching the floor while taking a shower. I didn't know any of that. I was scared to never be able to feel life outside the fight, feel alive in a more human way. And then you came. First you thought I was a Latina. And then you gave in when I asked you to teach me how to dance because I didn't understand at all what you were saying about your country's history. The next day I left Montreal and took your socks with me. One of them had a tiny hole on the toe and they were both worn out at the heel. I'd look at them and just laugh because our fight would continue moving forward thanks to a pair of old socks. It was absurd, completely absurd, and I couldn't stop laughing. The next day I saw my comrades again in a café in Frankfurt. When I saw them it occurred to me all of a sudden that we could make similar socks to both finance our organization and help circulate a political message. This may seem foolish, I know, but when you're drowning any log floating by looks good. Besides, I couldn't think of anything better to explain why I'd left with you that night, why I hadn't helped with other tasks. A week later

I found out that the organization had accepted the idea. I couldn't believe it. So we started looking for ways to make your socks, Alfgedó. You became part of our fight to create a Kurdish nation between the borders of Turkey and Iraq. When I got on that plane at Mirabel Airport, I thought about you as if you were the last man, the last human being in a world that was vanishing into smoke, distance, and our inevitable march towards death, Alfgedó."

At 7:00 AM on Wednesday, March 15, 1995, the small alarm clock made him jolt in bed, ripping him out of the dream world from which he was sometimes able to steal the fire of words and bring them into this world. Once awake, the chains of reality kept him tied to Memory Mountain while History Peak devoured his liver. CBC radio news informed that the ex-dictator, gonorrhal Luis García Meza, had been extradited to volibia from Brazil. He didn't move, decided not to get up, and let the news settle in the thunderous waters of his emotions. Listening to the news report, he felt knotty roots taking over his body and exploding in his abdomen, his nerves dissolved like molten lead and his body fell apart into silent weeping in relief. During the eight o'clock bulletin he was appalled to find out that the press had removed the update from the news block. Just like that. Had it been just an auditory hallucination? Something that had seeped from his imagination into the terrain of reality appearing to be real news on the radio? He got dressed in a haste, his ear pressed to the news. But they said nothing more. "Sonofabitch!" Back in bed, he couldn't decide what to do. He kept turning over and over like a screw for a good hour, trying to be as quiet as possible. Since he'd come home from the hospital, the few times he'd left the house he'd gone with

Bolivia's help—she'd go out wearing dark sunglasses and a scarf on her head like a character out of a 1970s Italian movie. Since his surgery he needed her even more than before: he only had one good eye since the incident with the Kurds; he'd lost depth perception and his field of vision was now reduced to a dangerously two-dimensional picture. Streets looked like colour photos and he couldn't tell distances between cars or between pedestrians. To make matters worse—and he hadn't mentioned a word of this to anyone, not even his doctor—something even more serious was happening. His right eye seemed to have declared itself autonomous and independent. It was functioning all by itself in complete disregard of the onerous task of focusing on shapes and contours that his left eye continued to perform. Choosing their words carefully, the doctors had explained that since his surgery his right eye had stopped working and he would never be able to see out of it again. However, throughout the day, at anytime, no matter where he was, he would suddenly stop focusing on the contour of things, and a movie stored in his memory would be projected, the way a dark room is suddenly lit up by a film on a screen. The beating he'd received in the Kurdish café had turned that abandoned eye orbit into a tiny movie theatre with a loop of thirty years' worth of images and stories stored in Alfredo's memory. It was rather disquieting. His irresponsible right eye, aided by his memory as an accomplice, seemed intent on destroying whatever was left of his mental health. It was 7:30 in the morning and Bolivia was sleeping beside him, her knees slightly bent, face partially covered by her hair. He kept reflecting on the events. He didn't dare to wake her up to explain the old gonorrhal García Meza's deserved prison sentence may have caused history to suddenly stop chasing its tail like a frantic dog in a park and moved forward a millimetre-long second. Perhaps now the word "volibia" could take on a new meaning. Perhaps this time history had at last succeeded in biting its tail and was about to devour itself and disappear. He walked out to the street and into the month of March. He headed towards Jean-Talon station, hopped on the metro and headed south to Sherbrooke station, where he walked up the stairs and out to the street. The day was clouded over Carré Saint-Louis—a small square that reminded him of Chuquisaca's main plaza. The fountain and the tree branches kept a watchful eye on the convalescent pirate walking across the square. He had a leather patch on his right eye, a thick winter coat he'd found at a garage sale, and a scarf about three metres long that looked like a black boa leash on an elephant. He walked down the three blocks of Rue Prince Arthur to Boulevard Saint-Laurent and took a left heading south to the Café des Virtuels. He ordered coffee with milk and drank it dipping an oatmeal cookie—although for the authenticity of the story, it really should have been a croissant, which is also called a *medialuna* or a *pan cuernito*. He sat on a bar stool and logged onto one of the public computers. An Argonaut in his quest for Colchis and the three-headed dog, he put a quarter in the slot and dived into the cybernetic mare nostrum looking for something to confirm the news he'd heard on the radio earlier that morning. Five dollars and seventy-five cents later, having crossed multimedia erotic promises, the valley of the hyperwhite Aryans, and the swamp of sadness of Celine Dion's friends, he finally found a news repository called 'Bolnet,' a rather flimsy portal (or rather, a small door, just a tiny mouse hole, actually) in a tiny corner of the Internet. He'd found what he was looking for. He entered a "p" for printing and then tore the news from the printer as if he were beheading three-headed Cerberus. The cable was succinct and uncompromising, written in short sentences. It said nothing about who had written it, but his one good eye was able to read that it had come from La Paz.

A bloody chapter in Bolivia's history has closed today with the transfer of former dictator Luis García Meza from a Brazilian prison to one in Bolivia, where he will serve a 30-year sentence. García Meza was received at the La Paz airport by hundreds of heavily armed police forces. He was taken to the Chonchocoro high-security prison, approximately fifty kilometres from the capital.

"I am innocent," he said as he boarded the Bolivian aircraft on Tuesday evening at a military base in Brasilia. A fugitive since 1989, García Meza was arrested in Brazil a year ago. The Supreme Court of Justice of the latter nation ordered his extradition last October 19th, but his attorneys delayed the implementation of the order.

García Meza, who is 64 years old, led the 1980 military coup that overthrew a democratically elected government, dissolved Congress, and banned political parties. The former general led the coup with support from cocaine traffickers, war criminal Klaus Barbie, and foreign mercenaries who assassinated, tortured and persecuted union leaders, politicians and journalists. At least 100 people were disappeared or assassinated during the coup. In 1981, he was forced to step down after the United States and other countries withdrew their economic aid.

The Bolivian Supreme Court judged him in absentia for 37 charges. According to the documents of the Supreme Court, he was found guilty and sentenced in 1993 for sedition, crimes against the constitution, genocide, fraud,

extortion and murder along with 52 former members of
his cabinet and regime collaborators.

He hadn't finished reading the last paragraph when his rebel
eye started making whirring noises. He was still sitting at
the café. Light filled his right eye and a projected image took
over the entire field of vision in his left eye: a scene with soldiers marching from one side to the other in an enormous
courtyard. Someone inside his head adjusted the sound, and
a voice he hadn't heard for 15 years began to read a poorly
written script peppered with impressionistic comments:
"… and in accordance with the Political Constipation of
the Bolivian State, I was enrolled in compulsory military
service—an absurd requirement that should disappear and
be erased from the nation's laws—in the Air Force Security
and Defence Unit, an air force battalion stationed in El
Alto, a few kilometres from La Paz. No experience is more
brutal for a seventeen-year-old than being recruited by the
Bolivian army.

"The morning of July 17, 1980, after a period of training
in local combat, our company became a service company
and was supposed to learn how to make adobe bricks. The
garrison walls were made of adobe, requiring a continuous
production of blocks to repair damages caused by constant
erosion and soldiers' nightly tactics needed for sneaking out.
Approximately at 10:00 AM, those of us fortunate enough
to own a radio heard the news report about the uprising of
a battalion in the Riberalta navy unit, in eastern Bolivia. In
previous occasions, a state of emergency had been declared
at our garrison, undoubtedly in preparation for this day. As
it tends to happen in those circumstances, the perpetrators
started the coup in small remote units in order to gauge
the reaction of larger military units and assess the potential

effect on civilians. Only then would a critical mass of the country's major military units be sent out to the streets."

Alfredo had stopped moving. He was watching what was happening inside his right eye orbit: in his inner eye the text was synchronized with the images in a movie he found both familiar and foreign. While mechanically lifting his coffee cup to his lips, he tried to convince his left eye to pay more attention to what the other eye was showing—it seemed more interested in reading the headlines on the newspaper a woman next to him was reading. "Lidia Gueiler's democratic government was undergoing tumultuous times due to the terror campaign the army had unleashed on the country. The climax of the period preceding the coup d'état was the brutal kidnapping, torture and murder of Luís Espinal Camps, a Jesuit priest and director of the weekly *Aquí* who was brutally hung up and tortured in the Achachicala slaughterhouse."

Stunned by the images in the movie, Alfredo dropped his empty cup on the table when he saw the Jesuit's slight figure running around Plaza San Francisco, wearing a woollen *chompa* and carrying his journalist's briefcase full of humanist ideas. It wasn't clear if the film narrator was aware that Luís Espinal had held mass in a small church in the outskirts of Villa San Antonio, that he'd given first communion to a group of teenagers who innocently believed in god in the midst of yet another military dictatorship and its war tanks. Alfredo recalled Luís Espinal in a classroom at Colegio San Domingo Savio, explaining the ideological mysteries of film to him and a group of film enthusiasts. The narrator's voice continued as the film ran twenty-four frames per second in his empty eye socket: "In the parliament, socialist writer Marcelo Quiroga Santa Cruz attempted to create a judicial precedent, seeking to put an end to decades of military impunity and corruption by prosecuting dictator Hugo Banzer Suárez, whose contribution to national history included nearly 300 Bolivian citizens killed in three days of combat in the resistance against the August 1971 coup. According to those seeking justice for the years of terror, 14,750 people were detained, tortured and exiled between 1971 and 1977, 84 murdered, and 69 disappeared, in addition to squandering the national economic surplus. During those years, members of the Banzer family serving as diplomats were expelled from Canada by the Royal Canadian Mounted Police on drug trafficking charges."

"With the news of the Riberalta uprising, tension invaded the El Alto air force battalion. No one understood what was happening outside. The atmosphere was tense. Anxious groups of soldiers congregated to listen to updates on battery-operated radios. Only a year prior, in 1979, Bolivians had survived another brutal military coup led by Colonel Alberto Natusch Bush—so successful that he was never held accountable, thanks to support from civilian sectors represented by his minister of foreign affairs Guillermo Bedregal, a vulture, a politician of the most sinister ilk. The army had caused almost 200 dead and several hundred wounded. Civilians in city centres had been shot from tanks and helicopters. Despite the carnage, the Bolivian Workers' Union had succeeded in paralyzing the country with an indefinite general strike. Heavy participation of the peasant population in the resistance against the military coup was the final blow to Colonel Natusch's regime, which crumbled within sixteen days after appointing General Luis García Meza as general commander of the army. This victory over *gorilismo*—the country's experience before 1980—had created a sense of security in the population that an attempt against the government could never happen again.

We started hearing the first voices denouncing the coup on the radio. University leader Henry Oporto was calling for the resistance to organize and asking soldiers not to obey the orders of the perpetrators. Ten or fifteen minutes later, our superiors confiscated our radios. We were isolated. We had no idea what was happening but it was already too late for everyone. After the failed 1979 attempt, this time the Bolivian army was carrying out a different type of coup, relying instead on paramilitary attacks commanded by Klaus Barbie, a Nazi war criminal who had served in the Banzer regime. The colononel recognized his service by granting him Bolivian citizenship and even a military rank as assimilated personnel within the *thanta* Bolivian army. Using methods perfected by Germany's *Schutzstaffel*, para-military groups moved quickly in ambulances and stormed the Bolivian Workers' Union in the centre of La Paz, where political and union leaders were gathering to organize the resistance. Several were shot and killed, among them Quiroga Santa Cruz, one of the most brilliant politicians in contemporary Bolivian history. Survivors were taken, hands behind their head, to the Palacio Quemado at Plaza Murillo. The first wave of the coup carried out arrests, attacks and raids in various cities. At noon, officers in our unit disappeared to hold an emergency meeting. The upris-ing of a navy unit in a remote village in the eastern jungle had grown and was devouring the entire country. Hours later, the military garrison of the second largest city—the eighth army division in Santa Cruz—had surrendered, which created a domino effect among the different mili-tary units. One by one they joined ranks with the perpetra-tors. At 5:00 PM that July 17th, our battalion commanders declared a state of emergency in our unit as a couple of Austrian war tanks reached our gates, sent as reinforcement

from the Tarapacá armoured battalion, about five kilometres from the Air Base. The rattled officers and commanders of the seven companies resurfaced in the courtyard. In
each block, officers summoned their respective squadron
commanders. No one used the word 'coup d'état'—it was
a 'state of emergency.' The armouries were opened and
FAL Belgian rifles and 200 7.62-mm cartridges were handed
out to each soldier. We swapped our kepis for metal hel-
mets donated by the United States military, and squadron
commanders were ordered to improvise backpacks with
bandages and other first aid supplies. Companies received
box after box of standard ammunition, special ammunition
for tracer missiles, and war grenades. By 7:00 PM, troops
from the Tiquina Naval Force had joined to stifle growing
resistance in urban areas. All branches of the Bolivian army
seemed to be keeping each other under surveillance: first
two tanks from the armoured cavalry, followed by entire
companies from the naval unit. In the name of esprit de
corps, the Bolivian ersatz generalcy stabbed the civilian
population on the back with yet another coup. The air force
courtyard was filled with army forces wearing green burlap
fatigues, naval soldiers in black burlap fatigues; ours were
blue. We all wore combat fatigues for combat against a
city, against a country, against an unarmed, outraged population. That afternoon gunfire bursts started echoing constantly and intensifying after dark. In the days that followed,
we lived and contributed to the horrors of the coup—generous, indiscriminate shooting, raids, seizing factories. We
heard rumours of dead soldiers. According to our superiors' version, civilians had offered the nervous Bolivian soldiers poisoned oranges. The University was turned into a
giant military base for officers and paramilitaries to carry
out the painstaking looting of everything they deemed

valuable. My company followed orders to quell any gathering of civilians, to take over public squares and storm churches where flyers were being printed to mobilise the resistance. We were cut off from any possible avenue of dissent, and superiors watching our backs didn't put down their pistols and machine guns for a second. We'd heard rumours of soldiers shot on the back for refusing to shoot a population whose impotence roared as they witnessed the assault of their liberties. We were under surveillance. City parks and squares became military encampments. At night we would go out in military trucks to patrol the streets, arresting *cholitas,* drunkards, beggars and partygoers, anyone who happened to be out on the street during curfew hours, while on other streets unmarked Ministry of the Interior vehicles circulated freely, no questions asked. Someone would simply roll down the window and shoot civilians to death. Even during the day, machine gun attacks were carried out against civilians from unmarked vehicles, such as the one at Villa Copacabana—it was the government's way to intimidate and stamp out any resistance from the population. Our company commander gathered a contingent of soldiers who knew the geography of mining areas. Many years later, in Montreal, I would learn that in those days of July of 1980, the planes we'd been keeping under close surveillance—planes that roared as they took off, heavy with point-fifty ammunition for their machine guns, each under-wing rocket launcher loaded with half a dozen bombs—went straight to attack mining centres, where locals had organized a tenacious resistance fuelled by dynamite and courage."

"No!" Alfredo screamed, startling other customers at the café as if a cockroach had just come out of one of his nostrils.

He wanted to stop seeing all of that. "Why didn't I do something? Why didn't I revolt? Why didn't I empty my magazine on them the night we went with Non-Commisioned Officer Juan Barrón to escort gonorrhal García Meza across the entire line of flight to the Prevención? Why did I have to participate in the rape of Boxeador's girlfriend? I should have done something, trampled and burnt the flag we worshipped every morning, in whose name and glory we murdered so many people. Dance a vigorous malambo on the trumpet that summoned our battalion every morning. Put eyeglasses and long hair on Eduardo Abaroa and put a joint in his hand." Alfredo's tragedy was that of having lived without realizing that his personal life, thoughts and experiences were part of a social scaffolding, that he was part of the collective history, of the life experiences of people with whom he had shared his life, way of thinking, decisions, indecisions and betrayals. He'd never been alone. He'd never been an island because the horizon of his decisions would always be part of that deep, silent river of his peoples' unwritten history, those he vaguely sensed were his people, removed from the corrupt stain of every instrument of power.

His right eye turned off as quickly as it had turned on. He noticed his coffee cup was empty. He looked at the time. His left eye was misty with tears, a fact he accepted without being overwhelmed by what in the past he would have interpreted as a sign of unforgivable weakness. He carefully folded the printed news of the extradition of the aforementioned subject and walked out of the Café des Virtuels. He was surrounded by people. The air smelled of bread, coffee, onions. The loud bang of a car crash reached his ears. He was now living in Montreal, hundreds of kilometres and centuries away from his first death. He could continue remembering every detail of the events on July 17, 1980, when gonorrhal Luis García Meza inaugurated a Reich that would last at least twenty years based on his calculations. Alfredo could have climbed on top of a bus and yelled at passersby on the boulevard that the new government had baptized his new military uprising with the ironic title of Government of National Reconstruction, that his master plan was for the country he ruled to survive on *chuños* and potatoes. Who even cares today about the rear-guard militiaman who ironically declared himself anti-imperialist the day cocaine started coming out of his ears? Who the hell cares about this story at all? No one. Absolutely no one. And yet, Alfredo felt he had to write it down. And if young people decided to reject him, at least the dead—those who left waiting in vain for a promise of better days, the promise of living in humane conditions, those who were gunned down thinking it was worth sacrificing themselves for others, for those who would follow—the dead will know they are remembered, that their memory is still alive. That we have learned something. Even if it's only not to forget so easily. Our memory belongs to everyone, to those who died and those who live with buried memories. Our memory belongs to this solid ground, the earth that supports a tree of days in an infinite present. Even if no one came close to his writings, Alfredo thought that by writing these lines he would fulfill his promise to Amelia and Boxeador, what they had requested of him in the midst of horror and whispers: they had wanted to remain in this world, even if only as simple characters in a humble novel, they wanted to feel the eyes, the breath, the imagination of another human being who moved closer to the faint mark their fleeting lives left behind. Alfredo realized all of a sudden his one good eye was crying again under the March sun.

He thought about the historical convergence of pragmatized memory, in the postmodern exercise of a virtualized, hypertransient past. That memory, those days are a nuisance to the present. Alfredo thought that the only explanation for gonorrhal García Meza's words—"I am innocent"—could only be an effort to negate, deprecate and caricature memory. Even though we are now in 1995, even though today is January 1, 2001, even though today is Tuesday, July 17, 2080, even though fifteen or twenty or a hundred years have passed, even though we are literally halfway around the world, the Plaza de Mayo grandmothers are still there, demanding justice while Argentinian military officials continue on their edifying task of training Central American armies. Command headquarters filled with the grey, unpunished vultures of the Chilean army are still there. So are the US military missions, a cancerous tumour in every country, training locals in their art of slaughter as well as importing their culture of instant forgetting, denying the past. So are the Ley de Punto Final, the pardons, and the purchased or imposed innocence in the great carnival of Latin American democracies. Alfredo felt a bitter taste in his mouth. "Maybe foam should come out of my mouth. I should write, 'I want to write but only foam comes out.' Volibia: the land of burning foam. Is this triumph? Is this justice? It might be. Volibian law is famous for its fickleness, corruption and venality. Maybe García Meza will serve his entire sentence. Maybe the years he has left to live won't be enough to atone for the number of months of July he deserves to be behind bars. Or he might feign illness, endemic amnesia, for example. He may be pardoned and be granted freedom. He may even organize his own political party and become a decent, noble political figure like that mockery of democracy ex-dictator Hugo Banzer.

"There are two heroic blades stabbing through the language of memory. The first is the reason that García

Meza stepped down. It wasn't because of an effective civil resistance or because the Bolivian elite had demanded it. Neither of these was true. Private industry, mining and agroindustrial sectors in volibia continued to grow during those years, earning profits, signing fake balance sheets, and exporting capital. That elite of important frogs, led by one who would later become President Gonzalo Sánchez de Lozada, did not find dictatorship objectionable. In fact, the so-called 'private industry' had always felt more at ease and protected under military regimes. It was only when the collusion between the dictatorship and drug traffickers had become too blatant that the US and their domestic shysters forced García Meza to step down. The other blade is the constant expurgatory edge of memory. To this day, in his cell at the Chonchocoro prison, former general García Meza still believes he is innocent, while thousands, millions of Bolivians lived and continue to live the deaths and terror of that month of July of 1980."

I couldn't do it. I couldn't get it up. It was my turn. The officers' voices howled, thunderous in my ears, and she was there, on the floor of a cell at the Prevención, at the battalion entrance the night of August 6, 1980. The woman had tired of screaming. She had screamed until she lost her voice and was now sobbing quietly, the hands Sergeant Vásquez had tied now seemed to have surrendered above her head. A lieutenant, two sub-officers and four soldiers had already been bitten, kicked, spat at and scratched on the face by the woman who now lay in front of me. Lieutenant Ustariz was bitten and received the deepest scratches, until he bled, and only after punching her face hard half a dozen times did he manage to force her legs to open. Now the lieutenant was bright eyed and laughing, his hand resting nervously on the .38 Ruger revolver in his holster. Get it over with, dammit! A good soldier follows orders! Do it for your country! Jump on the *chola*!

"At 11:00 PM, the sirens of all parked and moving tanks and military trucks would warn the civilian population of the beginning of the curfew. Anyone found on the streets between that time and 6:00 AM could be shot without cause anywhere in the country. The sombre wailing would slowly take over the city as fear watched from behind doors and curtains. In the distance, desperate fists rapped on a door that was taking too long to open. Silence would rise above the city for an instant, then faraway bursts of gunfire one after the other. Warnings. A bloodied body falling on the ground. Soldiers pushed and kicked doors in, sometimes found small family gatherings. They arrested aunts and uncles, a grandmother, young boys, didn't even let them finish putting their coat on. Entire wedding parties, bride and groom, musicians and guests would wind up shoved into military trucks at the height of the celebration to be put behind bars in the army guardrooms and yards. Amid panic, rage and shame, the couple would surrender to the idea of spending the first night of their honeymoon outdoors, trembling with fear and cold like two sad chickens on another planet, in a country that could not be their own. In the distance, again the sound of shots, bursts of machine-gun fire, a scream, dogs barking, silence.

"The war tank went out leading the convoy. During one of our night rounds in one of the outlying districts on the way to Río Seco, some courageous *indios* or *cholos* had managed to blow up a stick of dynamite as one of the tracked armoured vehicles was driving by. The beast wobbled like a giant scarab, opened its infrared eye, turned its turret and continued on its way punishing the daring civilians with brief bursts of gunfire. Three army trucks went out behind the tank single file. We rode around El Alto under orange street-lights that bathed deserted cobblestones in plazas and streets. I was sleepy. My helmeted head swayed with the rocking vehicle. A shadow was moving slowly, feet feeling their way along the street. The shadow stopped. Started moving again. Cautious dogs were sniffing around the corners. The trucks continued their advance. The shadow didn't attempt to run or hide, waiting calmly for our arrival instead. '¡Viva Bolivia!' a nasal greeting, followed by an awkward attempt to sing the national anthem, trying to stand up still and straight to avoid the inevitable arrest. The lietenant jumped out of the cabin. 'Get in the damn truck!' The poor drunk took a bottle of pisco out of his pocket, took a sip and offered it to the officer. 'Have a sip, *mi capitán!* I used to be a soldier too.' The lieu-tenant accepted the bottle. He examined it with disgust for a moment, then smashed it on the sidewalk across the street. The drunkard was about to blurt out, 'You fucking asshole, why'd you have to waste my booze like that!' but the offi-cer kicked him in the groin, 'I said get in the fucking truck! Two of you over there, come here and take this piece of shit!' Two soldiers jumped out of the first truck right away and managed to shove the man and his insults and complaints into the truck, where he landed curled up in the centre of the floor. A few minutes later he started humming a song by the band Savia Andina: '*Sombríos días de socavón, noches de trage-dia, desesperanza y desilusión se sienten en mi alma...*'[13] '¡*Silencio, mierda!*' someone yelled, maybe a miner's son. Another kick landed on his ribs, followed by a weak protest from the man: 'Come on, *che,* let me pssst sing a bit! Just a little song, why's singing so bad, *che?*' He kept singing: '*...más en la vida debo*

13 "Dark days in the mineshaft, tragic nights of despair and hopelessness in my soul..."

sufrir tanta ingratitud, mi gran tragedia terminará muy lejos de aquí...'[14] He stopped singing all of a sudden, perhaps to avoid thinking about the weight of death hanging in the air and the trucks of the night. He started humming a morenada just to himself, completely oblivious to what was happening around him, as if he weren't really there.

We arrived at the Ceja de El Alto. The cradle of La Paz was a vast starry field, as if the sky had keeled and turned its territory around until it kissed the earth. La Paz was still and bright, as if it were suspended in mid air. It was midnight and the air was hazy with calm and danger. We heard the rat-tat-tat of a machinegun nearby. The poor neighbourhoods were most generous with their deaths. During the day, the place simmered with people, the place where the Altiplano and the city met. From there, the *campesinos* would see the giant urban construction for the first time, and for an instant all dreams were possible: work, school, health. The city was a stunning vista backdropped by the snows on Illimani's massive summit and, drawn in the blue distance, the contour of its three peaks, whose terrifying silence sometimes devoured planes and human beings. Perhaps the mountain was about to devour the city itself. But the city was reeling in the aftershocks of a *plaza tomada*. There, before entering the city was a stop that welcomed an endless stream of toiling buses all day long—windshields adorned with romantic decals, bringing from the most remote Altiplano villages young Native Bolivians, *maktitas* with their *bayetas* and *abarcas* who would come out confused and dusty from the road, wonder in their eyes, white eyelashes, dry tongue. Now in the dark of night, a few of the same patched-up buses were waiting at the stop, likely waiting to head out on their first trip at dawn. There, amid

14   "But I must suffer so much ingratitude, my great tragedy will end far from here..."

141

jolts inside our military transport, we saw a cautious figure lightly knocking on the door of one of the buses. The *cai-manes*—how people referred to our military trucks—were at the spot within seconds shining their powerful headlights on everything. It was a woman. The lieutenant walked out of the cabin as a shadow inside the dark bus stood up and walked towards the door. Machinegun in hand, the officer and a few soldiers promptly ran up to the bus. The woman glanced at the driver with a nervous smile as he opened the door. "¡*Tío!*" she said with a voice like a dove trying to fly out of her chest, "how are you?" biting on the stone of fear with each word. "I came to see how you're doing before you leave on your trip tomorrow." The poor driver listened for a second, still half asleep, not understanding much of what the young woman was saying, but once he saw the army men running up behind her and the panic welling up in her eyes, he said in a haste, "Get in, *hija*! Get in quick. It's cold out there!" The woman hoisted her skirts and took a first step up reaching up for the driver's hand. "Stop right there, *carajo!*" the lieutenant cried out as they exchanged terrified looks.

"Don't you know it's illegal to be out on the street after eleven?"

"*Sí, mi capitán,*" the driver answered, "but we're leaving for Pulacayo early tomorrow morning and…"

"I don't give a shit where you're going! This woman was out on the street and we're taking her back to the station. She's under arrest."

"Please don't, *mi capitán*, she's my niece and she's travelling, too. She lives far away."

"Oh yeah, let's see, is it true this is your uncle? What's his name?" the officer asked the woman, who had said nothing up until then, paralyzed by fear and uncertainty. She didn't know what to say and stared at the driver, her anxious eyes trying to decipher what his name was.

"His name is…his name is Julián…"

"Julián who?" the lieutrenant insisted. "Julián Perro, Julián Piedra, tell me, what's his last name, pues?"

"His name is Julián Apaza," the woman replied, trying to instil confidence in her tone of voice.

The driver looked down and bit his lips, then looked back up at the officer, sensing the inevitable. His voice dried up when the officer said:

"Let's see, Julián Apaza, show me your identity papers."

The sleepy soldiers outside were bracing themselves against the cold, tapping their feet on the rocks, the tyres, trying to warm up. They bounced up and down, rubbed their hands with their machineguns slung across their backs. The trucks idled outside with their lights on. The driver took out his identity card. The lieutenant asked him to turn the light on in a commanding voice that grew heavier with every question and made it hard to breathe in the confined tension inside the rural transportation bus. He examined the ID, then looked at the young woman, whose eyes were glued to the floor.

"True, your uncle's name is Julián…"

The woman sighed quietly, feeling deep relief in her chest.

"…but he's not Apaza. His name is Julián Calahumana, you fucking liar! What's your name?"

"Genoveva Ríos."

Julián Calahumana the driver, the drunkard, two students, three workmen, and eight soldiers from my company are outside, running around the perimeter of the large honour yard at the Air Base, driven by sticks when they fall down or when fatigue trips them and they roll on the ground. Every once in a while they scream and complain, but it goes on and they keep jogging, sweating out alcohol, fatigue, impotence, sweating their Bolivian condition on this dawn on August 7, 1980. We are inside this cell, nine soldiers and a lieutenant, in front of the crumpled body of a woman with her hands tied above her head. The lieutenant supervises, gets excited, orders, gets excited again. An entire squadron and Sergeant Vásquez have taken turns on that body. Soldiers who were unable to penetrate the body are running outside, being beaten from time to time. "That's what they get for being faggots!" Lieutenant Ustarez yells at them every so often. It's my turn and I can't get it up. She is still crying, her lips swollen, blood reddening a corner of her mouth, one of her eyes buried under bulging eyelids. I try to think about women, about breasts, thighs, about all the situations and experiences I still haven't lived but can imagine. I only see shadows, screams, shootings, people lying on the ground, photographs of the fallen at Ñancahuazú, bloated, naked, perforated on the front page of *Los Tiempos* newspaper. I see nothing but *caimanes* loaded with corpses headed to who knows where. Not for one second does it occur to me to take my rifle, gun them all down, starting with the general, majors, captains and lieutenants, even though I only have twenty rounds. No, it doesn't even occur to me, and because of this, because of this silence, I am guilty. We are all guilty. Speeches—from the balconies at plaza Pérez Velasco, from the university atrium—made believe there would be armed pickets all around the city aiming at resistance and victory. Guilty, those who proclaimed long life to democracy self-defence committees and left it to the construction workers and labourers to put their bodies between bullets and democracy. Guilty, those who stayed home waiting for the people, a people, some heroic, imaginary people from some leaflet to go out on the streets for us, to resist like a ghost army we are not part of. Guilty, we who waited for the mythical revolutionary left to defeat the new alcoholic order of gonorrhal García Meza. But none of that crossed my mind at that moment. The skirts had been tossed to the side, except for one that had been conveniently placed under her trembling, frightened body and the rammed earth floor. Her dark-skinned legs were spread—where they met, a glistening pubis with little hair where several men had emptied themselves in a few flapping, violent seconds. There were bloody splotches on her groin, and she kept crying and flailing, trying to free herself. Lieutenant Ustariz—a bloodied Christ commanding "Love thy neighbour," his knees raw from his carnal attack on the earthen floor—was starting to become impatient. With a smack to the back of my neck, he tried to knock me down to the floor, get me closer to the victim. "You're lucky, stud! So many out there would wish they could take your place. Come on, *maricón*... Are you gonna fuck her or do you want a fucking beating?"

The driver Julián Calahumana was panting like an asthmatic locomotive. Seventeen of us soldiers and four civilians were running with him—our punishment—dragging our feet, urged by blows from a few sergeants posted at the corners of the yard. Around 4:00 AM the driver fell down again and collapsed huffing and puffing, unable to move again. They called Lieutenant Ustariz over only when they realized that kicking him wouldn't get them anywhere and he couldn't actually stand back up. The man was barely breathing when the lieutenant reached his side. Calahumana tried to speak, to not suffocate: "...and...to think...my father...died...

fighting…in the…Chaco…War…" He was quiet again. His face had turned blue from heart congestion as the pan pipes in his heart stopped playing and his heart stopped beating the drums of a frantic sicuriada. They rushed to load his body into a *caimán* and took him to his old bus. Following the officer's orders, they sat him up behind the wheel in the same vehicle he'd been sleeping in a few hours earlier, waiting for the right time to leave for Pulacayo, the remote village he would never reach now. Genoveva Ríos, half naked, bleeding and unconscious, was dumped at the entrance of a public hospital. Genoveva Ríos, Boxeador's girlfriend. At 9:00 AM on August 7th, the seventeen soldiers who hadn't succeeded in grafting our anguished flesh between her legs the night before were now in punishment position, standing still like lampposts on top of a stone wall in the centre of the main yard, at attention, hands pressed firmly to our thighs, trying to balance and contain the fatigue that pierced us one bone at a time and set our bodies in a dangerous swaying motion. Lieutenant Ustariz, dark shades hiding the bags under his eyes, flaunted a war medal on his face from Genoveva Ríos biting him on the cheek. He explained to Major Trifón Echalar during the morning's first formation that our punishment was due to a mutiny attempt the night we'd failed to obey a superior's orders. The officers cursed, words came out like smoke from our battalion commander's mouth, approving our punishment. "You have to hit them hard. It's the only way they'll learn to be good soldiers." Later that day, soldiers from other companies gave us commiserating glances as they walked by our wall of scorn. Little by little, the punished soldiers started falling from the punitive height as they lost their balance, defeated and thrust against the ground by fatigue and the weight of their eyelids. They fell down one by one like sacks of potatoes, like downed trees, twisting ankles, injuring elbows and heads. Some struggled to get back up and walked their stiff legs to the building where they would try to dress their wounds, apply ointments to recover from the effects of a roaring night. Others did their best to stay awake, some crying and encouraging themselves. A concession. That was exactly the goal of the punishment: to humble you, break you down, shatter your spirits, make you guilty, make you accept that the penalty was just, make you feel like a piece of shit, like a worthless monkey. You are nothing but a mangy monkey, a little monkey that obeys the rigours of the stick. "Subordination and determination... Viva Volibia!" Even when you're out, as a civilian, you will still be a little monkey, you will continue to respect authority, the uniform, you will remain shackled to fear and accept in silence when they beat you and shoot you down in the name of the *thanta* volibian republic. That's why compulsory military service ought to exist forever. To get you used to obeying, so that you won't protest. You are nothing and that's why fear inhabits you, that's why you take refuge in your individuality, making you more and more fragile. You are nothing but a simple soldier. You are nothing. Your decisions are worthless. You can't do anything. That's just how it is. That's the way history is. Final stop. You are boliviano, *un buen liviano*, a good lightweight, an incomplete fuck, an obedient, patriotic half-fuck, proud of your manipulated tricolour flag: red yellow and green.

Laugh, laugh, laugh. I laugh on top of the stone wall that's meant to defeat me. I laugh at the flag, at the official bugle, at the national anthem. I laugh at the immortal guano that heaps star upon star on the martial shoulders of the great volibian army, undefeated conqueror of retreats and *corralitos* at Villamontes, heroic in Tolata, Epizana, mining centres, Chapare and the tropics. Laugh at the poor officers who joined the army betrayed by their stomach, by hunger, because in volibia only a uniform could guarantee access to the monopoly of power and fear and the spoils of war—the right to housing, food and education for their children. Laugh at their petty ambitions, their long study nights before they are tested on showing new ways of shooting at peasants or skinning cats. Laugh at their little stars, their little stripes, their little parachutist badges, their little courses on sadomasochism at the school of condors. Laugh at their honour, subordination and determination. Laugh at their little symbols, at their well-intentioned forgetting that the glorious condor on the national coat of arms belongs to same family as carrion-feeding vultures, at their primate pride and gorilla insignias in a country where chimpanzees have more humanity than the entire General Staff. At their love of shields and badges. Laugh at the lyrics to their anthems. Laugh at their honour guards, their little soldiers dressed in red at the gates of the Palacio Quemado. Laugh at their freshwater admirals and rubber ducks, their rearguard generals, their colonels in slippers, their dipsomaniac captains. Laugh about the *thanta* volibian army and its twenty-two thousand, thirty thousand, fifty thousand or one hundred thousand soldiers forced to enlist by the political constipation of the state or by hunger, so poorly dressed, undernourished, always beating or being beaten. Laugh at their Sunday military rituals, their uniforms and their drunken outings to Paseo del Prado. Laugh at their grim racism, their veiled homosexuality. Laugh at their rattling scrapyard aircraft, their sickly *caimanes*, their tanks bought at a backhanded discount. Laugh at their pig-headed servility when receiving scraps from the US Army. Laugh at their battles, at the foolish resistance at the Boquerón bunker, laugh at bugleboy Mamani who should have left everything behind to play his trumpet at the festivities of his hometown instead of winding up dead astride a useless cannon. Laugh at this kleptomaniac, alcoholic, jingoistic army. Laugh my heart out at the glorious Volibian Armed Farces, at the Suckling Forces of a country governed by tie-wearing roundworms, thieves with diplomas from a foreign university. Laugh at history. Laugh out loud, laugh the high military command into confusion, laugh your heart out because laughter frightens away tears and makes death less deadly. Laugh about this little stone wall. Laugh about this punishment. Laugh about this uniform. Laugh, laugh, laugh...

Remember that night when Boxeador's fists were weaving in the air, menacing knuckles, spinning slow, regular circles in the dark. Say it was the night of August 17th, when Boxeador died, when we found pieces of his skull encrusted in the wooden beams holding up the roof at guard post number eleven—or was it sixteen?—and we found his brain mass scattered in all four directions, whitish grey gelatinous blobs splattered on the walls and crisscrossed by tiny veins that looked like they were still throbbing. A fist whooshes by seeking someone's face, yours, as an explosion of enraged bats rises up, fists sink into your ribs, flatten your nose, unleashing torrents of blood and swelling up your eyelids. You take the impact. In one blow time falls flat on the ground, stopped, retinas burst. In one blow you hit the ground, the same night Boxeador singlehandedly knocked out half a dozen soldiers who'd been guarding the gates of the Prevención for eleven nights in a row, the same night they brought in Genoveva Ríos. Remember this because the dead only die for good when no one remembers them.

Remember Vicios, feeling his naked bleeding gums, feeling around for his teeth on the Andean soil, his ribs threshed and crumpled on a hillside of the Altiplano that echoed and resonated like a drum with each blow, each body that fell on the ground. Remember Boxeador's blows falling on you, mixing with sweat, blood, saliva. Remember his hands rising up to his face from time to time to wipe away his quiet tears, and then return to yours, even more vicious now, more accusing, because you were there, too, at the Prevención eleven nights ago, and you didn't do anything to change the course of events, because you were just one more witness, helpless and ectoplasmic, watching as the dirty, bloody sex of every officer and soldier penetrated the flesh of Boxeador's girlfriend, Genoveva Ríos. You cover your face, hunch your back, your feet tap the ground looking for balance, trying not to fall on the ground, trying to explain you're not to blame even though you actually are. You're to blame for every bomb in the mines. You're to blame for every death on every street. You're to blame for every single second of July of 1980. Guilty of having obeyed the political constipation, guilty of having obeyed that little poster on the wall calling that year's first echelon of recruits to duty. Guilty of believing in the Patria. Guilty of worshipping the flag. Boxeador is now a storm pouring fierce hail upon your back. You duck another punch and then—not minding your effective dodging and English guard, how tired your feet—with one tearful scream Boxeador flattens you on the mat of the Altiplano with a right hook to your face that resonates inside your skull like mortar fire. The film is erased for fifteen, twenty, a hundred years. Complete darkness. You are no longer there.

He woke up one night around 4:00 AM. He was thirsty. He went to the bathroom, emptied his bladder and drank a glass of water. When he turned off the light, there he was, in the half-light, half a metre away in front of him: Boxeador's silent figure in his apartment on Rue Cartier. He felt as if someone had hooked each one of his hands to a 220-volt live wire—every hair on his head and body standing on end. The apparition had a tattered bandage covering a large part of his head. He could sense the figure exhaling grief, frustration and pain, contained rage into the air. Alfredo tried to explain why he was writing about him, why he'd decided to interrupt that long silence of almost twenty years, knowing he should have consulted with him somehow before setting out to examine what had happened at the El Alto garrison that night in August 1980. But he felt his knees buckle under him, his throat full of rusty nails, his tongue a flap of dry hide. He never thought death would make Boxeador's figure so cold and imposing. He thought he'd explained his points out loud but hadn't heard himself say anything. As light returned to his left eye, Boxeador's shape gradually faded away in the darkness of his right eye. Alfredo had another sip of water. Outside, only the street lamps were still awake. Once again he scanned the white walls, the corners, the doors inside his apartment. There was no one there. He turned off the bathroom light and went back to bed, where Bolivia—the Kurdish woman—was sleeping, breathing in long sighs. He looked at the line of her shoulders, the motionless stream of her hair. He reached out to turn out the light but changed his mind. He stayed still for a moment, unable to sleep, his brain flooded with voices and images. He got out of bed again. He walked to the living room barefoot, turned on a small lamp, sat at his table and began to write again.

"The dead are never dead," Amelia whispered, walking up to him from behind. He was thinking about Boxeador. He didn't dare turn around to look, both startled and amazed at the welcome freshness of a voice that hadn't lost its sweetness with the passing of time.

"Today you inhabit the dead," she whispered in a tone that seemed somewhat celebratory. "Do you think about me sometimes, Alfredo?"

By way of answer, he wrote: "Your body, sometimes as dense as the silence with which you touch me. Under this sun that's almost never ours, you speak in the voice of so many voices and populate my fingers. Today the dead will speak to me about their shoes and their affections, and with their quiet, dusty love they will deny the fall." Behind him, she may have been reading what Alfredo was writing down, as detailed as he could, about all the sensations Amelia's presence aroused in him. He felt her rest her hands on his back, barely touching him, and heard her say:

"And then you realize our dead will also inhabit my voice. They, who never really left."

"Your voice?" Alfredo asked.

She glided towards the middle of the room and spun around, her feet not quite touching the wooden floor that now reflected her glow. She was wearing her thin green cotton dress again, the long dress that at seventeen had showed him the contours of a woman's body for the first time. It was that year's last dance. In the centre of the great hall at the Miraflores school, Alfredo was stunned noticing the exquisite shape of Amelia's body for the first time. She had somehow remained invisible to him until then—he hadn't known how to look—and now he was suddenly feeling the pull of giant magnets under his skin, volcanoes erupting in his chest, eyes and hands and lips. He couldn't look away as she danced in front of him, saying farewell to seventeen, farewell to the Hugo Dávila Secondary School, farewell to the quiet affection he'd felt growing inside him, climbing up like a plant through his fingers and ribs all those years, lacking the voice he would have needed to get close to her, to pour on her palms the ocean of words that churned inside him like an endless storm only she could stop with her breath, her voice, her masterful touch. Amelia kept spinning and spinning, filling the large gymnasium with whispers, laughter and music, the bright-coloured spotlights in the corners lighting up her steps, her lines and her movements in a long waltz of farewell to innocence. Alfredo's astonished eyes danced with her, feeling that month of September would never leave him after those last moments together, unaware that a few months later the light in her eyes would be extinguished forever while a phone rang in vain in another room. Perhaps she would have answered Alfredo's call in those last seconds, but Death was mightier than the seventeen-year-old woman's vigour. Since then, he would never stop dying—endlessly, one word at a time. Now, twenty years later, Amelia was wearing her green dress again, spinning and taking him on paths where past, present and future intermingled, erasing all reference points, all borders from which to return, all traces of identity. Now Amelia took on Marcelle's features, spoke to him in Marcelle's voice, reminded him they'd be meeting up again tomorrow at the Champ-de-Mars metro, near the ticket booth, right by the Montreal map, to go for a walk through the halls of the Château Ramezay, stop in the middle of the seventeenth century, look in colonial mirrors that may still recognize, hundreds of years later, that recurring game a man and a woman's hands play to verify they exist, hold each other by the arm to enhance their vital sense of breathing one more afternoon on the streets of Montreal's Old Port, and then, once the night had lit up the city's luminous pulse, walk up Boulevard Saint-Laurent to drink the night right out of the bottle, followed by sweaty shipwrecks and panting silences, an attempt to bridge the distance that lay between them before they'd met, across walls and deserted rooms in the old house where Amelia was confined, watching the days being built. "Write, Alfredo, write all of this down!" But he just listened to her, unable to tell whether she'd betrayed him—her, the woman who could become every other woman at the same time as soon as he called at the gate of the colonial house of time and oblivion, asking to see her and her signs and references. Amelia would come to see him after walking through several patios, hallways filled with books no one read anymore, past the fountain adorning the centre of the patio of arches—identical to the Condes de Arana house in La Paz. Sometimes she managed to sneak out of the house of the dead without being seen, and she would come to surprise her author, who sat drinking cuba libres surrounded by cumbias and jaranas, practising in vain how to fully surrender to the exercise of forgetting in some remote northern island.

"Hey, would you like to dance?"

"Yes," she whispered, "and I'll also tell you how you're going to die."

"You and your morbid jokes!"

"You know me, Alfredo, so take it however you like while we can be together. You know? My existence on paper, this madness for life I was unable to feel or touch, and that's now taking me over, it's all possible only because of you. I am right here in front of you. I didn't have to go to the station to find you when you thought you'd never see me again. I've seen that we, the dead, love life with such eagerness that even underground we'll seek anything that's filled with its own life energy. We flower above ground, become moss on rocks from so much tenderness, turn into a leaf just to feel the wind, disguise ourselves as dust so we can travel, hide in people's minds, embed ourselves in the bones, the imagination, the memories of the living, and we only really die when people stop knocking on our door to ask us out on a walk, when no one utters our name anymore. That's why I want to tell you when you're going to die. That way I'll be able guide you, show you how things are, show you ways of living even after death, show you that darkness is just another form of light. That way you won't be alone, Alfredo…you won't be alone. Alfredo, you will die after thirty-three years of love."

Alfredo stood up while she kept whispering in his ear. He started spinning around, unaware he was alone in the early morning hours, dancing with an invisible someone in his arms. In the intimate darkness inside his right eye he could see Amelia's face, her long hair, her bright eyes, her glistening lips. His left eye was closed to the world outside. Music was playing and Alfredo was dancing to a waltz that with a little luck would never end. But fatigue and time finally won, and he went back to sleep next to Bolivia's warm body. She felt him get in bed and, asleep, reached for his hand and brought it to her sleeping sex.

The grey March sky has gotten under your nails and chilled your blood. It snowed last night and today you have to watch your step, jump over huge puddles of ice and snow that have begun to melt. Your feet are cold. The month of May will never come. You see one of the city's small red snowplows along the sidewalk removing the last of the snow. Dirty, stubborn, sticky snow stuck between freezing and melting. You walk into a café for shelter. You eat something that vaguely tastes like cooked vegetables. Probably the *soupe du jour*. You avoid the ice cubes in your glass as you drink your water. It's cold. Thick winter coats, faces wrapped in scarves, hands in gloves, tall boots splashing slush as they walk by. Hurried steps, focused eyebrows. March is a long waiting room. Then, as if the light had descended upon you, a woman turns onto this street—a sudden heavenly deity, a messenger sent by the warm sun in late June. Something about her doesn't quite match the month or the snow or the grey sky. She's wearing a short skirt that reveals the cadence of her forms warming the air as she walks by. Graceful and strong, she fills the street with the sweetness of warmer days to come. The skin awakens to touch, touch awakens to warmth. Life's drum beats loud and strong. A solar flare of skin and a lunar knee suffice to lull cold to sleep until the end of the world as your chest blooms with the buzz of other seasons—leaves, lips, songs. A woman you don't know and will never know, whose slow steps you'll never see again leaving a trail of overwhelming beauty, and these long winter months of forced cold and Mediterranean nostalgia simply vanish. As she disappeared around the corner, Alfredo thought his endless admiration of the feminine words, gestures and forms was a sign of an early decline, a foreshadowing of the dirty old man he would one day become. Besides, it wasn't politically correct to find in a woman's body an absolute and valid reason to keep loving life, or was it? Alfredo examined his sausage-like fingers—a sign of sedentary comfort?—with his empty eye, which had become his own personal movie theatre, covered while in public with a black leather patch that made him look more street-smart. He was glad his left eye still worked and could revel in shapes, light, skin and clouds, as well as the silence and darkness that dwelt in his right eye socket like a blind, tender spider. He started scribbling down in his notebook the first thing that came to mind, without stopping to think twice, and felt like the only thing missing right then was learning how to smoke properly.

They lay side by side under the covers. "You know what we did with your socks, Alfredo?" Bolivia said with her head on his arm as. "First I hid them in my handbag and took them from your apartment that morning. Then I brought them to Ankara with me. People in the party there thought my idea was interesting, though they made fun of it at first. They realized right away we wouldn't need a big investment and besides, everybody needs socks. They're not expensive to make or to buy. We could use what we made from selling the socks and other symbols to finance our publications and presentations. That way we'd have money to rent theatres and show films, cultural exhibits and dances in Madrid, Marseille, Montreal. We could pay for our posters and communiqués, buy computers and fax machines, make long-distance calls. But soon we realized we couldn't open our small factory in Turkey. It would have been suicidal. In those days the government had stepped up their efforts to persecute our movement. To this day it's illegal to be Kurdish in Turkey, you see? You can't be who you are. It's against the law. You can't be yourself, you have to be something else. I thought about you so much, I thought of writing you, asking how things were in Côte-des-Neiges, ask you to have a ceebu jen on Avenue du Mont-Royal for me, Vietnamese phô at Jean-Talon. I had never felt so free, so alive in any other city before Montreal. It's a shame we didn't get to see and get to know one another longer. Ah, these times! Anyway, first we took the small factory to Nuremberg, that old German city where Hitler held his gigantic Nazi military gatherings. But our project didn't take off there either. There was too much hate, too many bombs against immigrants. There was a wave of setting fires at immigrant shelters. They were attacked even where they worked. For the first time I was seeing Turkish people crying for their dead, for the first time they felt and reacted like we did when they persecuted and killed us on Turkey's streets, near the border with Iraq. I understood then why they practise against us what they endure themselves. It's so absurd. It's a simple matter of historical memory. A bit like what the Israeli state does against Palestinians—the Jewish people have forgotten what it's like to live once you've been ousted from your land, to be murdered for resisting occupation, to be accused of your own ethnic origin. In Nuremberg and all over Germany, the Turks and all immigrants felt cornered, against the wall, not knowing which night they'd be getting a Molotov attack through the window, or which one of their children they'd grab first to escape a fire. I couldn't tell anyone in the organization, but for the first time I felt pity for Turkish people. They'd been living in Germany for generations, but they would never be seen as equals. So I washed your socks with a little bleach and put some cornstarch on them so they'd look cleaner and newer than they were. I took a few photos and sent them to our people in the United States to see if we could open a small factory there, a co-op of some kind. And they said yes, that the PKK people could take care of sock production, but they'd do it south of the border, in Mexico. And that's when I told myself you'd definitely had some part in the course of history. So your socks went to New York first, then to Frankfurt, from there to Ankara, then southern Turkey, to Nuremberg, again to the United States, and finally Mexico to die a business death. I remembered that night we danced together, and I asked you to teach me how to dance, to speak to me in Spanish. I had never made love in Spanish. Did you think I was an immigrant hunter? Silly, if I'm an immigrant myself, and from a country that doesn't exist. You never said if you enjoyed sleeping with me. Did you?... Yes? Really? Since I didn't speak Spanish, I didn't go to New York or to the factory on the Mexican border. I stayed in Germany a few more months working on translations, participating in presentations, organizing soirées and lectures. Then I went back to Marseille to see some friends. Why didn't I go back to Kurdistan? First because it doesn't exist, and because they killed all my people there. I have no one left there. No one is waiting for me aside from people in the organization, and probably Turkish intelligence agents. That's why I thought I'd come back to Montreal, because I liked the idea you might be waiting for me. Were you waiting for me? No?... Yes?... Tell me the truth. The factory south of the US border started operating. Things started going better within six months. That's when we started getting more resources. We had more funds, and other parts of the organization were able to buy more weapons, supplies and ammunition smuggled from Czechoslovakia. Are you comfortable? is your arm asleep? hand me that pillow, am I really that heavy?...no, no, don't get up yet, we'll grab coffee later, it's my treat, but let's stay in bed a little longer now...of course I know Czechoslovakia doesn't exist anymore. Yes, yes, I'll explain the Colemerik bomb in a bit. After a while we noticed the remittances from the Mexican factory were arriving less and less frequently, even though we received reports that the factory had grown, that they'd started making other products. That's when bickering erupted among different factions of the organization. People in Europe wanted to expand the political-military campaign beyond the continent. Militants wanted to take actions to the United States because they're the main weapon and equipment supplier for the Turkish army, but people on the other side, in the United States, were fiercely opposed. They said the plan could risk the future of the factories, which were three now, and that the best thing was to drive our fight through more moderate means, make representations before the European Parliament, plead our case at the United Nations, file a lawsuit before the International Court of Justice, mount human rights campaigns in Turkey. It wasn't going to work—it had never worked. In discussions and debates we studied the Palestinian case, analyzed dozens of international resolutions and rulings that failed to advance Palestinian rights even a millimetre. We looked at the Nicaraguan case, too, and the International Court of Justice ruling. Am I boring you with all this? You want to me to go on or should we get something to eat? All right, go to the bathroom…I'll wait, but don't take too long, eh?"

"Should I go on?…yes? but don't fall asleep, eh? Well, we finally made a decision after analyzing the Palestinian experience and a really heated debate about the Bosnians, who were being destroyed by the Serbs. Some Bosnian contacts approached our organization, desperately asking for any weapons and ammunition surplus we had. You see, the Turkish government's propaganda had made them believe we had giant arsenals. The truth was we paid for every bullet and every rifle literally by taking food out of our mouths. We took advantage of those contacts and asked them to share their experience with international organizations. I've never seen so much bitterness, so much frustration and impotence together. The Bosnians were literally being exterminated in the name of world peace and welfare, basically because they are Muslims. So we decided to take our military campaign to the United States because the only language they understand is full body bags. That discussion we'd had made us realize that focusing our efforts only on negotiations would lead us to disaster and demise. There was terrible anger in the United States once we started our military campaign. We took over Turkish embassies in several European countries, bombed Turkish travel agencies in Germany, and then one day some members of our organization in New York were arrested and deported to Turkey. Someone on the inside had betrayed us. A few months later, the authorities sent some of the bodies to their relatives—fingers smashed, charred heads, lungs full of industrial oil, missing thumbs. We thought it was just a terrible coincidence. We didn't know it then, but the French police had arrested several Kurdish leaders in Paris. They had their address, phone numbers, even bank account numbers. The same thing had happened in Germany, Spain, Italy. I'd gone back to Turkey. I'd gone to Colemerik to take photos and write new accounts of Turkish repression. And then my cell received the order to pick up a vehicle already loaded with explosives and park it at the entrance to the Mustafa Kemal Hotel, two blocks from Colemerik's central square. We had exactly ten minutes to carry out the operation. The car bomb was meant to destroy the location where several members of Turkey's military intelligence in charge of operations in the area were. We were supposed to sneak back to Ankara to receive further instructions. We parked the car right outside the hotel and walked away quickly, as we'd been instructed, but not too fast so we wouldn't look suspicious. The bomb went off when we were only a couple of blocks away, after only three minutes instead of the ten we'd been told it would take for our own safety. The explosion was massive, Alfredo. We'd never been able to assemble a bomb with such power, so we thought it was really odd. There's no way we could have armed that bomb. We were a good distance away from the car, but we could see the thick cloud of smoke, phosphorus, nitrate darkening the sky. And then we started seeing fingers, hands, joints, pieces of metal and brick falling from the sky. You could even see tiny drops of blood like mist suspended in the air. Once we were back in Ankara we learned exactly what had happened: seventy-six people had been killed, and about a hundred injured. We had killed the members of our own leadership. Who'd given the order? Who'd prepared the vehicle? We learned later that our financial wing had informed on our New York comrades. They kept the factories, put the organization's assets in their names, and eliminated the few loyal contacts we had on the East Coast. The business sector of the PKK had intensified their efforts with a blind, murderous zeal. We should have known sooner, when they refused to abandon the sweat shops in Mexico. We'd proposed leaving the area because our movement was aimed at Kurdistan's independence, driven by the abstract and absurd but necessary ideas of freedom and justice. And there was freedom in those factories, yes, but it was such a bullshit freedom—people couldn't even go to the bathroom in peace. They argued that moving our production area would affect our income too much because the cost of labour would be so much higher. They wouldn't even consider it. Now it's too late for anything. The organization is bankrupt. We've been torn apart. We're wanted everywhere. That's why I came here. It was really hard to find a passport and even more to find you, Alfredo. It wasn't that easy, you know? But I knew they wouldn't find me if I was here with you. At least that's what I thought until they beat you up and sent you to the hospital. Now I don't know what's going to happen. But

I know they'll hold me accountable for what happened in Colemerik. And they'll find me guilty no matter what I say. They've already made their decision. They have to shoot me, take me out, eat a cold, disgusting plate of revenge, even if they die of an ulcer and regret. I had to cut off my hair. Leaving Turkey cost me a huge amount of money. I lied and said I was Spanish until I got out of Europe."

Alfredo thought whoever was watching him work on his little novel was still mad at him, standing in the dark, hovering over the island of light on the papers on top of his work table. In the past few days, Alfredo had learned how to get startled less easily every time Boxeador showed up. Sometimes his head appeared in the refrigerator next to the yoghurt. Others his mangled face would stare at him in the mirror with his one good eye while Alfredo was shaving. The first few times their encounters would turn into serious outbursts, but gradually they became quiet dialogues between one-eyed men. He thanked the gods and whoever had invented disposable blades for not having to use a straight razor to shave—he would have easily sliced his jugular in one of his terrors. In those moments of revelation, Alfredo felt he could almost breathe the sense of contained rage in his old comrade's look. "What do you want me to do, Boxeador? You want me to stop writing and abandon everything?" He just stared back, unmoved. "Are you ever going to stop coming here? Are you ever going to leave me alone? You could at least help me write this novel instead of trying to frighten me to death." He asked himself if it was even worth trying to communicate with the ghost. "I want to understand what happened that night in August, too, Boxeador." Pacing around his apartment, Alfredo continued his long, unanswered monologue, and started feeling more nervous—he was an amoeba under the microscope of Boxeador's gaze. He sat down in front of his papers again and started writing more quickly until he fell asleep on the table, head resting on his arms, overcome by fatigue.

Bolivia was sleeping when Alfredo arrived in his Rue Cartier apartment, north of Boulevard Jean-Talon. He took off his clothes in the dark and slid next to her warm naked body under the covers. After a brief, close skirmish during which he could barely contain the darts shot by Priapus—whose penetrating intentions were awakened by Bolivia's naked body—Alfredo finally fell asleep. He was dreaming. The dream grew and merged with the walls around him, which vanished and engulfed him in a world impossible to evade or ignore. When he opened his eyes, a soft drizzle of snails and spiders was falling from the spacious night above; every so often he'd have to shake out the covers, and the molluscs and arachnids would go flying into the air, then fall with a soft crackle on the floor faraway from the bed. After some time, the ejected creatures would get back on their feet, extend their antennae, uncurl their legs or ooze their slow slime and make their way back up the dark, invisible walls. Sometimes a sharper, heavier thud would reveal the presence of a spider as big as a hand that, defeated by gravity, landed on the three of us as we tried to sleep while listening to the night and its noises.

How long had we been there, in that place whose shape and boundaries we ignored, ruled by the deepest darkness? Sometimes we felt birdwings whooshing in that imaginary black sky. We could see our eyes and teeth glowing pale and moist in the dark. We were waiting. For what? A ship? For the light to come? For someone to arrive? Sometimes we'd kiss, unconcerned by the spiders or by what her mother may think of me—if she could see us. Bolivia would wrap herself around me, moaning, panting, until we fell asleep, almost sweetly, surrounded by the incessant insects. In silence, our hands had learned to recognize each other in the dark.

Sometimes you could hear a babbling, like a stream running down to the bottom of the space we were in, but none of us dared to dive into that deeper darkness. Once, we tried to calculate distances around us by throwing rocks to try to orient ourselves. We would toss a rock and wait to hear them land. But nothing came back. Only after a while, consumed by frustration and despondency, we would hear the faint echo of an object falling into the dark depths. Gradually we learned to talk less, to say nothing for hours and hours, for days on end. There was only a bed, an improvised mattress placed in what we thought was the middle of dark space. We could feel drafts of air coming from seemingly faraway, bringing smells that made us rejoice: wood and fish, forests and rain and freshly tilled earth.

We were waiting: she, her mother and I, who slept between the two women when I was tired. At the beginning, the mother wouldn't allow her daughter to sleep next to me. But the cold and loneliness caused them to make gradual, imperceptible movements to be closer to my body. There were days—days?—when we were able to see the snails on the uneven stone walls. Their movement was a strange form of writing in the dark, like slow commas in the space of infinite waiting. They were black like tar, darker than night, and their imperceptible movement drew whimsical, undecipherable phrases. Sometimes spiders would run and chase each other around, stumbling over the snails, which stopped on their tracks and hid under their spiral home or simply dropped to the floor.

We measured the passing nights by the fatigue in our bodies. In my sleep, as I often did, I started searching for the woman's warmth. She would tenderly welcome my hand between her legs (or at least that was the memory the dream had kept of its own existence). This time I met something unexpected—perhaps I hadn't paid enough attention, or something had altered the usual order of things. My hand met a hard marine shell crowning a pubis—that was not the daughter—as if a bird had made its nest in a glade. As soon as my touch recognized the rugged seashell surface, a fierce crustacean came out of the shell armed with powerful pincers that locked around my fingers until they bled. Through the silence buzzing in my ears, I could hear the hot liquid pouring out of my wounded fingers, pain numbing my joints. I could see her mother's pupils shining in the dark, staring with malicious satisfaction. She put the aggressive crustacean back in its place, where it rested standing guard over the bellicose pubis. She went back to sleep.

Later we were awakened by the hum of a distant horn, a ship we imagined filled with people, light and music.

During our long days of waiting, we would recite old stories and plots, or hum soft songs, almost to ourselves, to keep our minds busy and preserve any sanity we had left, until we started to forget all the stories and songs we knew. Our feet occasionally crunched on a snail as lost as we were in the unpredictable, constantly changing terrain.

We were sleeping again. I could hear the two women breathing on either side of me, waiting for something, or someone, or some event that even I couldn't foresee. After the last time I was savagely bitten, I was paying more attention to what my hands did in sleep. I was sleeping when a hand surprised me, searching for me. It grabbed my hand and placed it slowly on a seashell. I tried to wake up and make my hand flee like a bird from the pain I'd memorized would soon follow such an encounter. But none of that happened. The fingers guided mine lower, into the depths of a moist pubis that throbbed to the touch. My fingertips were soft in their touch, feeling lips that hid another smaller night, allowing themselves to be seduced. Gradually, first my fingers, then my hand, were pulled into a warm, silky ocean. I tried to adjust my position and, without being able to help it, my arm followed my hand, then my head, my shoulders, my torso, until my entire body was submerged.

Exploring that body from inside, I can still hear the distant snapping and crackling the snails make in their endless fall from the ceiling. In here, though, there is only water. There is no wood anywhere. Sometimes you can see rivers of small, brilliant red fish swimming by.

When he woke up he felt as if he'd just run his first marathon, exhausted and sweating from an all-night struggle in which he had to choose between history and oblivion. He looked for Bolivia but she was no longer next to him. She'd left a note: *"Mon Alfredo, Merci pour ton accueil et si tant d'affection envers moi. Je suis obligée à te quitter pour quelques jours, peut-être plus. Je ne sais pas. Je t'aime, mon gauchiste-caviar. Bien à toi: Bolivia."*[15]

It hit him as if he'd been beaten by a soldier, a cop, an Opus Dei priest and a Jehovah's Witness all at once. No! Not again! Elusive Bolivia had left once more. Maybe it was fear, that nasty, unforgivable fear that had driven her away again. What good does love do in this life anymore? A few sparrows were practising their little hops on the balcony. He stayed there for a moment, stunned. He got up and

---

15   "My Alfredo, Thank you for taking me in and showing me so much affection. I have to leave you for a few days, perhaps longer. I don't know. I love you, my poutine leftist. All the best, Bolivia."

showered, got dressed. There was a desert of grief in his abdomen, in his throat. Abandoned again, sad, upset, wounded, empty, tearful. He reread the note, tried to smile and cheer up enough to face the day, but all he found was a lump in his throat. He tried to convince himself that she would have never stayed with him anyway, that the fire of her cause and the terrible oppression her people endured would eventually prevent her from being with a man—in this case him. He said to himself over and over that her leaving was inevitable, their roads went in opposite ways, she believed in the construction of a patria while he was trying to free himself from the weight of his own tragic one. He grabbed a pen and meant to write something like: *"Mon aimée Bolivia, J'ai peur de te revoir parce que tu me quitteras à nouveau (au fond personne est à nous), et je le souhaite si tant. Dans un tiroir de mon bureau je garde une petite histoire écrite. Je ne sais pas si elle est vraie ou non. Je veux te la montrer. C'est ma façon de vaincre la distance et surmonter les pièges de la nostalgie. C'est une histoire pour nous seuls car maintenant je le sais : ma patrie, ma terre, mes mots, c'est toi, c'est ta voix, tes bras, tes paroles. Alfredo,"*[16] but he didn't write anything down because his pen didn't work, and he couldn't think of much to say— all he wanted to do was sit down in the corner and cry until he went blind. He walked out of his apartment, went downstairs and out to the street. The cold air dispersed the faint scent of gunpowder that had invaded his apartment—and his nostrils—since Bolivia had opened her suitcase and settled in. On his way to the metro, Alfredo began to realize he

---

16 "My beloved Bolivia, I'm afraid of seeing you again because you'll leave again (in the end no one belongs to us), and I want so much to see you. In a drawer of my desk I keep a little story I wrote. I don't know whether or not it's true. I want to show it to you. It's my way of overcoming distance and getting the better of the nostalgia trap. It's a story just for us because I know now that my patria, my earth, the words I write, are you, your voice, your arms, the words you speak. Alfredo."

couldn't live without her. What he needed right then was a quick suicide, to inadvertently be run over by a car, get hit by lightning, be devoured by little birds. After all, he hadn't forgotten Amelia's promise that she'd guide his steps after his death. He thought hard about Amelia, but she didn't appear anywhere. The best thing would be to stop writing for a while, let things calm down somewhat and start writing letters instead of stories—although this whole mess had started precisely when he'd decided to write a letter to Susana, the woman he'd met at the university's round plaza in La Paz, whose image would never abandon him. He kept walking towards Jean-Talon metro, became one more of the many passengers in a lifelong journey from the Ogowe Basin to the neighbours in Cochabamba, Pompeii and Marrakesh who travel through the underground bowels of this entire city riding its blue metal train. Doors open. Eyes, coats, daytime and evening hairstyles, mouths, trousers, Turkish tongues, shared air, sweat, and lotions. Shoes, sandals, winter boots. Someone is singing with an awful Neruda complex. You watch the travellers' eyes cross the air. They sense the presence of your pirate eye and take flight, rise above people's faces, lose themselves in the depths of ads for creams, cigarettes, baseball games, sanitary cloths and wines. Your voice attracts the attention of other metro riders, if not because of its tone, at least because of your tongue: Bolivia! Bolivia! Her absence is now a fierce ringing in your ears, a clamp around your throat, silvery fish fleeing from your tearful eyes in her search. Even if they don't understand you're calling out someone's name, they can at least tell you're looking for someone from one car to the next. You approach faces, features, familiar skin tones. Your nose searches for her scent. But your one good eye doesn't lie. It wants to be helpful and creates illusions that do nothing more than feed your despair. Bolivia is not in the metro. Bolivia is no longer in Montreal. You walk through doors from one car to the next through de Castelneau, du Parc, Outremont. You are Kurdish, Cochabambino, Montréalais. You are African, Arab, Vietnamese. You are everything and nothing. You are a tongue, a voice, a question that will never find an answer. *"Chunquituy palomitay... kolila!" Montréal est la première ville nord-américaine avec la plus grande population trilingue.* The olive-skinned ears of Tamils—escaped from Jaffna's fire and ambush—seek familiar phonemes. A Hindu thinks he hears verses in ancient Sanskrit as he drifts in a drowsy dream towards the west end of the city after washing dishes, pots, and floors at the Bombay Palace—the palace of succulent tandoori chicken and curry sauce—with soap and scrubber in his raw hands from one in the afternoon until five in the morning at a Sainte-Catherine Street restaurant. Dictionaries and history books no longer help. History doesn't exist beyond these pages. This is the history you breathe and sweat and weep biting your tongue in your hopeless search for Bolivia, crying out her name in vain, a name that means nothing to the people on the metro. Forgetting is a useless resource. The metro keeps moving. It pulls out of Université de Montréal station. You walk through another door, searching for a potential reader, someone whose firm fingers will know how to tie your personal history to the collective history, condemn the pragmatism of political convenience. You hate volibia. But volibia is in your tongue, your skin, your bones, your way of being and suffering and loving. You love Bolivia but she's no longer with you. You only have memories of being together on certain corners, walking certain streets with her, words in other tongues, memories of kissing, so many nights together. That Bolivia is no longer with you. The passengers feign indifference, pupils conceal their own curiosity, perhaps restrained reproach, disdain. Who are you? Something forgotten? No, I am laughter, a dog writing to the moon on a corner on Avenue Duluth. But even mongrels have a memory, don't they? *No, señora, yo soy boliviano. Boliviano...boliviano, volibiano...*ah! you're just another one of her lovers! Does it even matter if there are many of us who love you? An old song, a guitar tuning its strings in his imagination. Exhausted, he got off at Côte-des-Neiges station. No one had detained him. No one had asked for explanations or accused him of remaining silent in the past twenty, thirty years, of not telling anyone that the magazine in Boxeador's rifle had been full, not one cartridge was missing when you picked up his flaccid body, his soft brains under the stars in El Alto. You didn't say anything about that Mamani, either, or how they dislocated every single one of his bones. Or anything about Julián Calahumana or about Genoveva Ríos. They're not characters from our official history or from civics class. Over there, an impoverished man, the same one that appeared in the first pages of this book, recycles himself again as a recycler at the end of a story that has no head or tail. Like a country. Now the pauper is smoking part of a cigarette, a butt he found on the ground. Alfredo thought at least someone out there would understand the search behind all his words if not their purpose, which he had been unable to access despite the blood that ran through the underground tunnels under his skin. He imagined running into Bolivia, his Bolivia. If only to hear her voice again, her Marseille accent. To be Bolivian. To have a heart that beats to the rhythm of a national anthem set in a never-ending cumbia beat. To hell with volibia, the other one, over there in the south, governed by pirates armed with computers, learned thieves trained in foreign universities, inflated egos. Alfredo walked out of the metro and sat on a stone bench; memories of a movie he'd once imagined came rushing back. Right away his good eye threw its hands up in the air and went to sit on the substitutes' bench while the other eye socket, the empty one, turned on its invisible projectors. Sitting alone on the metro platform, Alfredo saw in his blind eye a woman walking out of a small apartment near the Jean-Talon metro. She boards the train and gets off at Sherbrooke station. She walks towards a café near the Carré St-Louis, the Café des Virtuels. She merges with pedestrians along Rue Saint-Denis—their way of walking, speaking and dressing hints at summer's imminent arrival. Colours are bright: It's around eleven on a sunny May morning. She walks across the Carré Saint-Louis to boulevard Saint-Laurent. Near the Musée Juste pour rire, the camera rises above the pedestrians in a wide-angle shot à la *Nuit américaine*, then stops facing the bar in a café packed with Internet surfers from around the world who drink coffee while typing hurried letters demanding explanations from the infinite memory. The woman notices she is being followed by the hero of the movie, a man who looks like he's from Cochabamba and stands there, stuck between hesitating and going for it, then finally sits next to her and asks the waitress for the same thing she's having, a Colombian coffee—the kind that reaches Canada despite the deaths and gunfire. Moments later our hero succeeds in promising the woman a century of love in a nearby room. She looks at the only spectator in the theatre as if asking him for advice. The camera lifts us in the air for an instant and then draws in for a close-up: a key to a lost paradise being handed over. The room is ready for the original sin. Bolivia's face looks at him from the screen and whispers only one name: "Alfgedó…." Frame by frame, the denouement fades out. Will they live thirty-three years of love? On the screen, as it slowly fades to black: *"Prochainement dans cette salle de cinéma."* His right eye goes dark. He can hear the metro roar as it approaches in the tunnel from the Siglo XX mineshaft. He opens his good eye, notices he's still in the Côte-des-Neiges metro, sitting on a polished black stone bench. Sitting next to him, a woman tilts her head sideways, struggling to read the title of the little book Alfredo Cutipa is holding: *Red, Yellow, Green* written by a certain Alejandro Saravia. When Alfredo catches her staring at him, she doesn't look away. Instead, she meets his eyes and asks him point-blank: *"Est-ce que vous avez fini votre livre?"*[17]

THE END

---

17   "Have you finished your book?"

BIBA VOLIBIA!
(Twelve pseudo-poetic attempts)

POEMS BY ALFREDO CUTIPA

**Mr. Ricardo Jaimes Freyre, please come to the
phone. You have a long-distance call:**

Ricardo, you brought me axes and horses
heavy shadows and deaths dancing
on points of ice and Nordic spears.

To the beat of drums of boiling metal,
you emptied rhymes over the sleeping irons.

Brief question in November about a dead man

Today: day of the dead.
I wonder what spirits my grandfather
Paulino Saravia Choquehuanca
is drinking underground?
to the beat of what music will his bones break?
under what silences of moss and dried flowers?

July 17, 1994

I have died of memory,
pierced by the iron,
the lead of forgetting
the nails of old images:
an officer inciting us, a diploma
for our brave sacrifice.
A chola shot in the forehead,
a dog with a crown of intestines,
a street where the stones
bleed out human salt.
For a long time
I have been living these deaths.

Colonel Muñoz,
blessed be the worms that guard you.
Major Trifón Echalar, don't you wake up some nights
with your throat filled with blood?
Captain Almaraz, mestizo steeped in hatred
are you still bullying your company
of ninety terrified boys?
Lieutenant Torres, does the patria exist?
what is this rag we swear allegiance to?
what patria do we use to justify ourselves?

The Salt of the South

Salt of tears,
salt of rage,
salt of love with skin unscathed,
salt of Sunday and chicken chanka.

The Illimani,
is it salt, is it sugar?
or is it only a solemn cloud,
barely clad in stone
to give weight to our dreams?

Sal...   Salt
salir...   depart
ir...   go
irse...   leave
ser...   be
Sur...   South
leave from these lives
sun that dawns south
drying the night, drinking the shadow,
drinking sun that leaves behind
the salt of its steps
on the crust of this earth.

In the south salt
is fire and lies
it is wrath and paths
it is desire and screams
it is crying and decrees
it is oblivion and entrails
it is living and leaving
it is death and word.

Brief reflection on the art of being Bolivian at four in the afternoon in Montreal on a Sixth of August

The wood is golden, like brown skin in the August sun.
The hours drink the afternoon
as it hangs its clouds and birds
out on the balcony.

It is August and I should feel patriotic,
tricolour and Bolivian.
I wait.
It might rain.
In Paris they drink wine at the Embassy
and a secretary says on the phone:
"just one thing… it's almost over" (you better not come)
To be Bolivian in August in Paris is to drink some singani,
run into some zampoña-wielding Andeans in the Odeon metro
to want to cry a little
and feel dry
like a river of burning stones
dreaming of some rain.

To be Bolivian in Washington
is to eat salteñas around ten
near the Ballston subway,
dance cuecas at night,
get drunk and feel like you'd die
to see Cala Cala again
and then sleep
under an alka seltzer moon.

The afternoon in Montreal
waves shirts and the ties with their fetishes
turn augural with starch.
In a hotel tonight
someone will sing at the top of their lungs a frog anthem,
and some will sit down and say nothing,
furious to be so boliches.

Then there will be chicharrón, beer
(imagined paceña)
and somewhere
someone will invent illegal chuños,
disguised locotos.
Perhaps to be Bolivian
is a matter of stomach.
To be Bolivian is to be a believing devil
eating fricassee
an anxious brown-skinned man, a melancholy Pepino.

Four in the afternoon
a forced time to want to feel Bolivian.
A little.

Approach to nostalgia

I look for another sky behind this sky when the air,
the first air, runs between my fingers again
coming down from the mountains.

I would turn this chest into a profane, beautiful, emphatic drum
"You're a philosopher,"
Too much hard labour and not enough food.
"Philosopher," the mestizo said to himself
on an Altiplano pierced by quenas and blood
soaking through a simple land
where bones become roots.

Horn,
pututu on the mountain, the one that terrifies those who believe
this is an ailing people.

Admire this beautiful jaw, the poetic traitor serpent,
that not of river or water, not of salt or tin
but of verse and Garcilaso,
of fog, swords and blazons
hides more than it shows and stills more than it sings.

This tongue, rustling softly, doesn't know—poor thing—
(nor does the mestizo, son of philosohistory and the assault
      on the flesh)
that underneath our learned skin,
—brown fish, blinded by so much salt—
there is another tongue, that of a world captured
by force of palace, grammar and good governance.

Sustained by the false rib of an armed Adam,
we awake as flashing devils, with oil-bearing mouth
and a sterile mineshaft, extending into the infinite void,
hanging between our legs.

¡Indio! You must insult yourself.
"That's what I've always told you!"

Cueca danced in August by Doña Memoria and Don Colononel, with bullet accompaniment

Who cares about the dead?
Who cares about
the wind split by an August of bullets?

They came for him on a Thursday.
At Regiment Bolívar de Viacha, they beat my father
hard on the knees with a metal pipe, until
butterflies came out of his wounds and his children's
faces floated in the air singing parts of Christmas carols.

It was Saturday when his colonel stars struck
and crushed the lips and skull of my cousin,
so close and so removed; photographs fell on the ground
invisible ones his brain had stored from so many birthdays,
of chairos and Sundays and lunch. No one could find
his missing eye. It has remained
in the air, floating in our memory.

In August they killed a teacher. He was found
with books in his intestines and on his lips agonizing
verses that will never return to Quebec.
He died kissing the stones, looking at this earth
and though already stiff, they kicked on and broke
the silence of his ribs, the dreamers.

On a Monday, de facto knives gutted an
Indian. Searching for gold, or perhaps silver, but they only found
a corn huayño waiting for the carnival of the year.
The chiwankos cried a golden yaraví,
but the colononel didn't understand he was setting on fire
among the Natives of Tolata the fertility of the earth.

When the fourteen bodies fell
somewhere in a cemetery whose name
no one cares to remember,
the colononel ate his boots, licked
his sated sex and became general
and the fourteen bodies, with eyes wide open,
their voices hoarse from so much screaming
cried flowers and candles
and turned off the night.

Who cares about the dead?
One hundred years of oblivion shine in the pupils
of the great General Hugo Banzer Suárez
and his useless artifices
of democratic vegetables.
Who cares about the dead?

Who cares
if his excellency
the post-candidate
former president,
neo-democrat made of cheese and military fang
has already presided
over the valley of death?

Long live democracy!
Death to the dead!

Eulogy to the photograph, the raincoat and the absent hat

To whom?
Who will be with me when a comet passes by?
Who will help me work the forge of words?

Not the snow captured in my bones.

Who with the blood and the oil
and the radical veins of the old people at the hour
of the main corner?

Not the black thorn of the naked vine.

This sun,
dry, primary knot
who does it belong to?
Not to the steps of Jaime Sáenz,
not to the beard
or to the migrant hat.
And the numb liquor?
And the paint brushes at dawn?
Where the fervour
of the seer reader
of leaves and misfortunes?
Who with crazy Borda?

Not the frozen pupil
of many a fallen star.

La Paz

You are cradle of the earth,
open, split,
devil's tooth,
Telluric sex
of water and blood like the furious rivers
that rush down from the Andes in February.
You are history of the earth
living your histories of inhabitants and stones
You are cradle of the earth:
llipta mouth and coca taste,
orcko voice and devil's grindstone.
Inhabited pachamama,
snow lluchu, Chuquiago,
llama hair scarf.
You are smooth, dry mouth
that sings in a voice pierced
by so much contained silence.
You are womb of the earth
in all the power of your fires,
your stones and your mosses.
Mouth of the earth,
inhabited by indios, anguishes and mestizos,
so dressed in bones,
so dressed in oblivions.

To you nothing binds me.
In you everything beckons me.

Morenada Dancers

(Dosage: your visual ingestion must be accompanied by the rhythm of a morenada or, if appropriate, by a saya yungueña)

Masks, long feathers as the morning clears,
fireworks, stones, people, dancers...
dance of the slaves! (and yet they're not slaves).

Splendid drum,
burnished indigenous morenada
in which mirrors and rattles tremble in one arm
with blind memories of black Africans and chains.
(Bones at the bottom of the centuries,
in the shipwrecked night of the planks,
breathing brine the Yoruba piled down below,
sowing the deep-sea trenches with panthers and spells
in the womb of the Atlantic fish.)

Did they speak Spanish, Portuguese, German or English,
those mouths that still chain, all of them nights from other
regions, all of them peopled by bronzes and whips, imaginary nights blooming now in the steps and rhythm of
indigenous people dancing now in the Andes, on the quiet
waves of a sea of height and straw?

Their bodies are filled
with rhythms and spells
miner's boots,
abarcas and rooted heels?

This is a morenada! Morenada of indigenous people and
mestizos with dreams of black Africans who were dreaming of spirits, birds, lions and rivers where time pours its
infinite flow before the final wreck.

They are gods, more than gods, Orishas no longer of the
    element of Heraclitus
but of absences in the air, Oludumare, Yemoja
veins of milk and thunder sunk under the earth
where no one comes by to draw blood from the seam
only Tío does, they say, but that's another rhythm and
    another erected god.

Be they gods, sad or slaves,
that's the dream of the black Africans of the Niger
of the waters asleep at the bottom
dreaming now a dream of salt
in which they are Indians, they are dust
dream that it's tomorrow, the rattles are clattering
and they are dancing an Andean morenada.

There are masks, long feathers,
costumes, fireworks and bands.
Dance of black Africans! (yet they are not black Africans).

First variation on an imagined
encounter with Tarijan music

"Porque van diez años
que dejé mi tierra.
La gente me mira
con ojos de ausencia."
"Because ten years have passed
since I left my country.
People look at me
With the eyes of absence."

"Don't say
you don't remember me," I will say to you.
By the first ice-cream seller,
don Alonso de Mendoza watches us
captain of stone and peninsula.

Time is the sabre of silence.
Under Calle Potosí the imprisoned river runs,
the devalued throat of the centuries.

La Paz under a government of
burning flies,
San Francisco of the broken faith
the cholas in the silpancho trench.

You don't remember that gate, on Evaristo Valle,
the hallway at midnight,
where my hands,
blind fireflies
with urgent veins,
populated the constellation of your shoulders
and your modesty
fell asleep in my wild tenderness?

What will I say to you?
I know.
Here is my photo (a blot of stamp and ink).
A bad photographer,
a passport, sea salt.
Our incomplete farewell and hurried old age
No? Doesn't ring a bell?
What do you mean?
You don't know me?
But if it's me!
no?
Ah! well, I'm sorry for the confusion,
I just thought you were…

To the happy few that rule volibia

(Also known as the government, the elite, the bourgeoisie, the rosca, the thieves, the milicos, the gringos' bootlickers, the oligarchs, the mafia, etc., etc., etc.)

Scab, puddle of important frogs
with a green, English-speaking beamgod
apes, elegant decadent cows
with a kleptocratic thirst burning

in their bellies bursting flags.
Ah, paisanos bovinos y livianos
important men with wallets
almost american the bolivians

who lick as modest as an appendix
the rifles, decrees and laws
the civil architects use to steal.

Their thanta viceroy democracy
box, paper, pencils
so easy to plunder, like saying yes.

ABOUT THE AUTHOR

Alejandro Saravia was born in Cochabamba, Bolivia, and lives in Montreal, where he works as a journalist. Saravia is the author of eight volumes of poetry. His trilingual (French-Spanish-English) poetry collection *Lettres de Nootka* (2008) has been studied in various Canadian universities. His most recent book of poems is *L'homme polyphonique* (2014). Saravia has given readings at the Havana Festival of Poetry and Art, the Blue Metropolis Festival in Montreal, and the Rhythm and Colour Festival at Harbourfront Centre in Toronto.

ABOUT THE TRANSLATOR

María José Giménez is co-director of the *Apostles Review* in Montreal and assistant translation editor for *Anomaly* (formerly known as *Drunken Boat*). A poet and translator, she has received fellowships from the National Endowment for the Arts, the Banff International Literary Translation Centre, and the Katharine Bakeless Nason Endowment. Born and raised in Venezuela, María José studied at universities in the United States and Canada, and currently lives in western Massachusetts.